GW00870073

Liam

They were out of the barn and into a bigger yard. In one corner was a small sty that Liam hadn't noticed before. Inside it was one of the smallest piglets Liam had ever seen.

"Maisie's runt," Roy said. "Noah wanted to have it put down but it's rare and lively. Might grow up to be a dwarf, but if you'd like to have her she's yours."

Liam looked at her, unable to believe his eyes. A pig of his own! She would grow, of that he was sure. She was a minute miracle, from her tiny trotters to her mobile ears and the bright eyes that stared at him unwinkingly.

Also available in Lions

The House of Secrets

3

Liam's Secret

Joyce Stranger

Lions
An Imprint of HarperCollins*Publishers*

First published in Great Britain in Lions in 1994
Lions is an imprint of HarperCollins Children's Books,
a division of HarperCollins Publishers Ltd,
77-85 Fulham Palace Road,
Hammersmith, London W6 8JB
1 3 5 7 9 10 8 6 4 2

Copyright © 1994 by Joyce Stranger

ISBN 0 00 674829 5

The author asserts the moral right to be identified
the author of the work.

Printed and bound in Great Britain by
HarperCollins Manufacturing Ltd, Glasgow

Conditions of Sale
This book is sold subject to the condition
that it shall not, by way of trade or otherwise,
be lent, re-sold, hired out or otherwise circulated
without the publisher's prior consent in any form of
binding or cover other than that in which it is
published and without a similar condition
including this condition being imposed
on the subsequent purchaser.

Liam's Secret

CHAPTER 1

Today ought to be exciting. Today he ought to be able to do everything he had ever wanted. Today ought to be marvellous.

It wasn't.

Nothing was as he'd expected. Liam Murray had thought that this day would be the most wonderful day in his life and, in most ways, it was like any other. His expectations made it worse.

Today he was thirteen. Today he had entered into a new world, the teenage world that his brother and two sisters had inhabited for so long. They seemed to have enormous fun, while he lagged behind them, unable to do any of the things that they did because he was too young.

As he went downstairs the phone began to ring. Let it ring. It was never for him. Nobody answered. They must be busy with an animal patient, or had an emergency.

He picked up the phone.

"House of Secrets, Veterinary Surgery, can I help you?" he said, imitating Romana Lee, who always answered like that. Romana was a gypsy woman. She had become a veterinary nurse, working with his father. She lived in a wonderful old caravan in the woods.

"House of Secrets," the mynah yelled. The voice at the other end of the phone sounded amused.

"Liam? That was Jed, wasn't it? It's Roy. Are you busy? I could do with some help. I've an emergency."

Roy Marsh lived two miles away, on the other side of the lake at the bottom of the garden. Easy to cycle there. Liam wanted to see Roy anyway, but if there was trouble, he'd never get the chance to ask.

"I'm not doing anything. I was coming over anyway. Can Troy come?"

"I don't like her running beside your bike, and nor does your father. It's too dangerous. I know it's quiet round here but Georgie was

8

knocked down on our narrow lanes. Can anyone drive you over? She could come then."

"They're all busy and Grandma's gone shopping."

"Then she'll have to stay behind, I'm afraid. I do need you here."

Liam often helped Roy. It was much more fun than anything else he did. He wrote a note and pinned it to the board on the kitchen wall.

"Roy rang. Needs help. Back for supper. Liam."

He switched on the answerphone: if they were all busy the bell just went on ringing. Nobody could stop operating on an animal to pick up the phone.

"Busy, busy, busy," croaked Jed in a weird voice. He began to shrill like the telephone.

"You'll drive us all mad," Liam said. Jed barked at him. Troy barked back and Liam covered the cage, which always silenced the bird. He could almost feel Jed sulking in the dark.

He shut Troy, his brother Bran's German Shepherd, in the kitchen and was conscious as he rode off of her forlorn face at the window, reproaching him for leaving her behind.

There was a pale blue sky and a faint sun. It

9

had been a wet summer and looked as if rain might catch up with them later. The lanes were puddled from last night's downpour which had been so heavy he had been woken by it drumming on the roof.

The school holidays would soon begin. Lucky Georgie and Bran and Jenna, who didn't ever have to go back. He wished, more than ever, that he wasn't the youngest in the family.

He turned the corner of the lane. The five-barred gate facing him was half open, the field empty. Had there been stock there? He had seen no sign of straying animals. He dismounted and closed the gate, wondering whether he ought to be looking for a missing flock. Beyond the gate stood a lone rowan tree, its berries already beginning to turn orange. Beyond that were two haystacks, the old-fashioned kind that almost nobody built these days.

Roy hated the polythene-wrapped bales, saying they were an eyesore, that there was too much of the beastly stuff around, and that it was environmentally unsound. He also used horses to pull his plough.

Had Garnet and Sapphire and Emerald and Pearl been in this field? Liam had a sudden vision of the four massive Shires marching into the village. Better get up to the farm fast and find out what had been there.

He sped into the lane that led to Brydale Farm. The distant hills were sheathed in a mist of cloud. He cycled between two fields where pigs grunted and grazed and lived free. As God intended, Roy said.

Long ago they roamed everywhere and were driven from places like Norfolk to London to be sold, taking days on the journey, foraging as they went. It must have been odd to have farmers driving pigs, or cows, or geese, or sheep, along the roads to market.

"Does them good to forage and be free to roam and have to hunt for their food, instead of being penned indoors and having it put down in front of them, with no incentive at all for living." That was one of Noah's favourite speeches. He helped Roy.

For all that the sows came indoors when they were heavy with babies, a week or so before the little pigs were born, and they had the best of care.

"Just as well Roy never married," Liam's father often said, after a visit to the farm. "He'd never find time to even say hallo to his wife." Roy was older than Josh Murray, his hair grey, but his eyes and voice and his movements were all young.

"Never had time for a wife," he often said. "Too much to do and never leave the place."

Grandma thought Roy was the original perpetual motion machine. He never seemed to sit down and everyone wondered if he ever slept. His farm was a showplace, kept by only two of them. Noah, the pigman, seemed as old as his name. A little gnarled man who found immense pleasure in his stock, Noah was as agile as his employer and had a fund of strange stories that fascinated Liam.

"Know how they cured whooping cough in the old days?" he had asked Liam on his last visit. Noah's youngest brother, Joseph, had died of the disease, though nobody ever seemed to get it now.

Liam shook his head.

"Pass the child nine times over the back and under the belly of an ass. Happen they'd done that to our Reuben he'd have lived."

He had bustled off with a bucket of pig feed.

Roy had laughed.

"Happen our Reuben would have died of being kicked by a donkey," he said. "Can't imagine old Skit standing still during that process." Skit had been retired long ago and stood forlornly in one of the paddocks, longing for someone to come and talk to him.

Liam had visions of parents queuing to treat their children, while old Skit fussed and fretted and misbehaved.

"Probably gave the poor kids brimstone and treacle too," Roy said. That sounded disgusting, but Noah then produced an even worse recipe which included mouse tongues. Liam began to list the remedies in a notebook. It was fun to tell his friends at school about them and see their faces, especially the girls.'

He stopped to look as he came to the orchard. Rack and Ruin, the two Gloucester Old Spots, came to greet him grunting happily. Roy named them because they seemed to spend most of their time digging in the paddock, wrecking it. Noah said they were hunting for truffles, only there weren't any there for them to find.

"Make a fortune if there were," Noah said.

Liam rubbed their ears. They were old friends. They were massive animals, creamy white, with black spots on them. Their pushed-in noses wriggled at him, and their immense forward-pointing drooping ears almost hid the bright black eyes that regarded him with pleasure.

Rack grunted companionably. Liam always felt the big boar was trying to tell him something important. He had a variety of sounds, and sometimes his tone seemed to be that of a question. He followed Liam along the fence.

The pigs were busy clearing up the fallen apples. Rack caught a glimpse of red in the grass by the fence, and lumbered off and rooted until he could rescue his treasure, crunching it noisily.

"Got me an idea," Roy said, appearing from nowhere, and making Liam jump. "Only it's a secret, see. Not even telling Noah. When he's down at the Fox and Grapes and has had a drink or two his tongue gives everything away. Never trust Noah not to tell."

"What's in the haystack field?" The empty field was worrying Liam. "The gate was open."

"Nothing. It's for hay. Did you shut it? Good. I don't like gates being left open. Makes folk think they can use the fields as they like. I've even had families drive their cars in and set out a picnic on the grass, flattening it and making it almost impossible to cut. That one's due for cropping soon. It's the last of them. Left it late, because of the rain. Noah and I have plans for a couple of really fancy ricks. People pay to come and see them."

"You said there was an emergency," Liam said, as Roy continued to stare at Rack and Ruin.

"There is. Wanted to wish you happy birthday personally and not on the phone. And got something you might like. Something special."

He led the way past the two big barns, where chickens and geese and ducks wandered between the big pens that housed the breeding sows. Hay bales were piled high, with kittens playing around them. Roy seemed to have kittens all the time. The cats kept the rats and mice away.

Liam followed, wondering what Roy could have to show him. Something special. It could be anything. Or nothing.

"There," Roy said, as they came across the yard. He pointed. "What do you think of that?"

CHAPTER 2

Liam looked across the yard.

"Had an idea," Roy said, stopping at the end pen. "Well, a number of ideas." The sow that looked up at him was smaller than the rest, her bristly hair the colour of a rusty fox. She pushed her snout at Liam, who scratched it thoughtfully. "Bet you don't know what that is?"

Liam grinned. His father had given him a book on pigs for his birthday a couple of years ago. It was so well read it was almost falling apart.

"She's a Tamworth," he said. "Going in for rare breeds?"

"Going in for mind-reading?" Roy asked.

16

"Well, it's not a breed you've had before. You said people pay to see the ricks. So they'd pay to see unusual breeds, wouldn't they? Dad reckoned you'd have to diversify to bring in more income, the way farming is now. Nearly everyone else has. Nothing in farming pays the way it used to."

"You learn fast, don't you?" Roy said, grinning.

"I hear farm talk all the time," Liam said. "Dad says there is no one like a farmer for moaning. Is business really as bad as all that?"

"It's up and down," Roy said. "We aren't getting the prices for bacon and pork pigs that we used to get. There are so many restrictions and regulations, and also I'm in an environmentally sensitive area and need to think about conservation. I have to make up my income somehow. What made you think of rare breeds?"

"You don't have a wife to run a farm shop. Rare breeds seems like a good answer. It's what I'd do."

"Is it now? So I suppose you won't want your birthday present from Noah and me? She's not rare."

Liam stared at him.

"My birthday present?" What had Roy bought him?

He led the way into yet another barn, this one full of strange-looking machinery. The farm was a warren of buildings and Roy used most of the barns as short cuts to somewhere else.

"Farm museum," he said. "Been working, both of us. Collecting and putting it in order. Surprising what you find on other people's farms, put away and forgotten, sometimes for a century or more. Maybe not for this year. It's too late for that, but to start next Easter. Wondered if your Jenna would do us a favour and do us some signs and notices. Pay her, but can't afford much."

They were out of the barn and into a bigger yard. In one corner was a small sty that Liam hadn't noticed before. Inside it was one of the smallest piglets he had ever seen.

"Maisie's runt," Roy said. "Noah wanted to have it put down, but it's rare and lively. Might grow up to be a dwarf, but if you'd like to have her, she's yours and so are her piglets, if she does ever come to full size. Have to pay for the boar, mind, and do it all businesslike."

Liam stared at her, excitement bubbling

inside him. A pig of his own. Never mind if she wasn't a rare breed. She was full of life and energy and her bright eyes considered him inquisitively.

"Might be a pig in a poke, mind," Roy said. "She may not survive. I've never seen one as small as this before."

The piglet was a miniature, so tiny that Liam wondered if she could live, but she came eagerly to greet them, and sucked vigorously at the bottle that Noah, appearing suddenly, conjured out of his pocket.

"Afraid the others would squash her," Roy said. "They're twice her size and she wasn't getting anywhere near the milk bar. Born yesterday, and I didn't know what to give you."

Liam looked at her, unable to believe his eyes. A pig of his own, even if she was smaller than any piglet he had ever seen. She would grow, he was sure of that. She was a minute miracle, from her tiny trotters to her mobile ears and the bright eyes that stared at him unwinkingly.

He must look like an enormous giant yet she had no fear and nosed his hand trustingly as he bent down to scratch her miniature snout.

Her little body and hide were rock hard. She

finished the bottle with a great sucking gulp, squirmed free and came to look at Liam with a thoughtful expression.

He felt as if he would never stop grinning. A pig of his own. A pig that would grow into a sow and have piglets that he could sell, and buy more pigs. If Roy would let him have the space. Perhaps his father would let him have a corner of the orchard to build a sty. There was room.

"I can't take her home, we've nowhere for her." The worry surfaced suddenly. Did Roy mean him to take her away?

The little animal squealed forlornly as they left her.

"She stays here. Noah made the sty as his birthday present to you. We've piles of old wood from derelict buildings we've pulled down, so if you want to expand you can build the next sty yourself."

Liam hated woodwork. It never turned out as he wanted and he always banged himself or cut himself. Roy looked at the boy's dismayed face.

"We'd help. But you might as well learn something useful. Never know what will stand you in good stead when you grow up. I'm builder, carpenter, electrician, motor and tractor mechanic, as well as often half a vet, or my bills would be so large I'd go out of business."

If everyone were like you, my father might be short of work, Liam thought, but didn't say it. He might have said it when he was twelve, so he was growing up. The thought filled him with sudden exultation.

"The sty's great. Thanks, Noah," Liam said with such heartfelt appreciation that the old man flushed and grinned, totally embarrassed.

"She's lonely," Roy said, as the squeals followed them. "But the others might smother her, by lying on top of her. Maisie won't have anything to do with her and pushes her away."

"I wanted to buy a pig for myself. I was going to ask you if you'd let me. I've got sixty pounds," Liam said. "Just from my birthday. I've some savings too. There's nothing else I want. Can I buy her a companion?"

"Well, now. I wonder what we've got that won't be too big? Know what breed she is?"

"She's a Large White." He laughed. "She's the smallest Large White I've ever seen." The forlorn cries had called them back to the sty. He looked at the merry little face, with its big ears and pushed-up snout. She snuffled happily at him, delighted to be noticed.

"Large Whites are the backyard pigs they used to have in the mill towns. Factory workers bought them and fed them on household scraps and always had a pig for Christmas. Good doers, they are." Noah, who had joined them again, grinned happily and bent down to scratch the small nose. "Me dad always had one in our backyard. There were ten of us. We never went hungry though he was out of work as often as in. Didn't do much except beat for the shoots in the season."

He sighed and straightened up.

"This won't get the baby washed," he said, and bustled off, pushing his fingers through his bush of grey hair so that it stood straight up, giving him the oddest expression.

Greg, the big farm tom, pushed against Liam's legs, wanting to be stroked. He was an enormous cat and father of most of the kittens that grew into barn cats and kept the rats away. His handsome tawny fur was mottled, dark and light colours alternating, and his bushy tail was tipped with white. One ear curled where he had argued with a rival, and kept the scar.

He purred noisily as Liam rubbed his undamaged ear.

"Maybe I have just the right one for you."

Roy had been sitting on the edge of the rail surrounding the pen, thinking. "Only, if they're put together Noah and me will have two to feed instead of one, as we'll have to take the other right away from the sow. She won't have it coming in and out for feeding when it's been taken away from her. So maybe you can find time after school to come over and do some work with them. Like cleaning up and supervising their food. Your pigs. Your jobs. But we do understand about school. Important, that is. Can't have you staying away."

He led the way across the yard again and lifted out an almost newborn black and white pig.

"Cost you fifteen pounds," Roy said. "Company for the little one. What'll you call them?"

Liam cuddled the small pig. A Berkshire was rarer than a Large White. It kicked against him, and he almost dropped it.

"Is it a male?" he asked, and then, as Roy grinned at him, looked for himself. It was.

"Porgy and Bess. They both sound piggy," he said.

"Might not like one another," Roy said. "You can't always mix piglets from different litters. Have to sedate them to stop them fighting. We need to stay and watch till we're sure they are OK together."

Liam watched the baby Large White greet the newcomer. After a few minutes they snuggled up against one another and slept.

"No problem. Been lucky there," Roy said.

Noah had followed them. His little crumpled face looked at the pigs with approval before he walked briskly away.

"Now for lunch," Roy said, leading Liam into the big farm kitchen where the table was laid with crusty bread and cheese and farm butter and a huge ham. The two men lived mostly on sandwiches and only had a hot meal at night when all the work was done.

Noah stayed on in the evening, preferring the farm and Roy's company to his own overcrowded house. There was always a ham or a chicken or a piece of pork to cut from.

A big bowl held tomatoes which Noah grew at home.

The old man brewed tea that was so strong and bitter that Liam found it hard to drink. When they had finished eating and Liam was sure he hadn't a corner spare for anything else, Noah produced a cake tin and opened it with a flourish.

Happy Birthday, Liam, it said, in icing letters that surrounded a small model pig.

"For you to take home," Noah said. "My Alice made it for me when I told her what a big day it was for you. A real teenager at last." He grinned a gap-toothed grin at Liam. "Big day."

"I didn't know Noah had a wife," Liam said, when the old man had gone back to his work. Even though Liam had always known Noah, he had never spoken much about the past.

"He did, a long time ago. Alice is his daughter. He lives with her and her family. Three boys she has. You know her husband, he delivers your milk. They moved in with Noah when his wife died. His house was bigger than theirs, but even so it's a squash. I've offered him a room here, but he feels Alice would be hurt if he did that."

"Bruce the milkman," Liam said, surprised. "I knew he had three boys. John is in my class at school. Jerry is the same age as Bran. He got a scholarship to medical school. I didn't know Noah was their grandad. Don't know the other."

"Joe. He's the eldest. He works at Brook Farm, across the valley. You know them. They use your dad for their Jersey cows."

"Dad's favourite herd, but he says their bull is beastly."

"Jersey bulls can be devils and Moses is one of the worst." Roy laughed. "Charlie Dutton uses biblical names for all his animals. Got Jezebel and Samson and Ruth and Naomi. The last bull was called Nebuchadnezzar."

Liam glanced at the clock. Another couple of hours at least before he need go home. Grandma had planned a little party and it wouldn't be fair to be late for that.

He helped Roy stack their dirty crockery in a bowl of boiling soapy water in the sink.

"Soak till this evening," Roy said. "You learn to cut chores on a farm and save minutes." They went outside again into the yard.

"Joe hopes to get a grant to agricultural college," Roy said, continuing his train of thought. "They're bright boys. Noah's bright too. Didn't get the chance in his day. Not like now. Better put that cake tin in your saddle bag, or you'll forget it. I've some eggs for Grandma Bridie too." He settled his cap more comfortably on his thatch of hair. "Time we fed your youngsters, and then I'll share my secret."

Liam held the bottle for Bess, who tugged at it with delight.

"Soon be off that," Roy said. "Little pigs learn to drink from a bowl far quicker than any other baby animal."

It was turning into a much better day than he had expected.

CHAPTER 3

Roy led the way out of the farmyard into the lane. Some hundred metres away was an old cottage where Noah and his wife had lived. It had been empty since Lily died. Behind it was a row of stables which had almost fallen down.

Roy turned in at the garden gate. There were only memories of past flowerbeds, with nasturtiums and poppies rioting among the long grass.

"Going to do it up and rent it for holiday-makers," Roy said. He lifted the latch of the little gate that led to the stable yard. "When we've time. Noah and me are always chasing the clock."

Liam stared. Gone were the ramshackle buildings that he knew, replaced by a row of new stalls, better than any he had ever seen. Four shire heads looked out at him. Emerald and Garnet, Pearl and Sapphire. He went over to stroke them. Pearl, who was dapple grey, dipped her muzzle to his pocket. Roy laughed and produced four apples.

Garnet, chestnut with a white blaze, took his gently. In spite of his size, he was a very sweet horse. Emerald, who matched him except that she had a star on her forehead, leaned over greedily and snatched. Sapphire whinnied, afraid she would be left out. She, like Garnet, was grey, but her mane was much darker than his.

Sapphire loved making faces, possibly because she knew that made people laugh. She lifted her head, opened her mouth and stretched her lips in a demented grin, revealing a set of yellowing teeth.

"You're a nut," Roy said, pulling the long forelock gently. "That's one of the silliest party tricks I know."

Sapphire whinnied softly, and Garnet answered her.

"Good job I've no neighbours," Roy said. "People complain about animal noises these days, though heaven knows why. When I stay with my sister in Birmingham I nearly go mad. She's not far from the M6. The din of cars and lorries never stops: gear-change noises, engines whining, hooters blaring, brakes squealing, air brakes hissing, doors slamming. It's like being in the middle of a lunatic asylum. Give me my old rooster. There's a splendid noise."

Caper, the big cock, was likely to decide it was morning at any time of the day. He usually began his calls around five, but had been known to crow in the evening. Sometimes Liam wondered if Caper were shouting at the ginger cat who was apt to stalk him, though Greg would never have dared to attack.

As soon as Caper stood still and gave tongue, Greg fled.

There was one stable behind the row, standing on its own. That hadn't been there before. The others had been strengthened and smartened. This was newly built. Liam looked at it and then at Roy, wondering what was in it.

"What do you think?" Roy asked, opening the door.

Liam stared at the dainty mare, who stretched out her head to greet him. She was the most beautiful animal he had ever seen.

"Meet Kazra. I shouldn't have bought her.

It was wicked extravagance, and in these times it was a gamble, but there's no Arab breeding round here, and I've already sold her foal. His name is Haroun. He'll be going in a year's time. Not yet."

He held out a finger and the tiny animal cavorted, jumping on all four legs. He danced delicately towards Roy and sucked the finger. When Liam moved, the foal shot away, retreating to the darkest corner of the stable.

Liam didn't know how Roy could bear to part with the little creature. He stroked the mare's dark mane. Huge eyes, long-lashed, stared at him, and her ears pricked forward as he spoke, listening intently. Her slender body was the colour of creamy toffee. Her long tail was the same colour as her almost black mane. Her coat shone with health.

The foal was darker than his mother, the small body still so thin that his ribs showed. His knees and hocks seemed out of proportion, lumpy on the long slim legs. Haroun was curious about these people, yet afraid at the same time. He came forward doubtfully, then skittered away, hiding behind his mother, who turned to nose him gently.

"He's only a few weeks old. Still very wary

of people," Roy said. "I think that her first owner was probably rough with animals. They both shy easily. My horses never do that. Kazra will have taught it to her baby."

The mare was tugging at her haynet.

"She's the first Arab I've met," Liam said in awe. He had never seen so beautiful a horse. He adored her, every inch of her. He was almost ready to change his allegiance from pigs to horses, but the thought of Porgy and Bess made him sure his life lay in another direction.

"Has Dad seen her?" Josh Murray loved the Arab breed.

"Not yet. She only came yesterday. She's been at the stud farm all this time. A friend of mine owns it and he kept her for me till the stables were ready. I don't want anyone to know she's here. She's valuable, and you know what a lot of trouble there's been over horses being hurt lately. I walk her after dark, when no one's about."

"You can't keep her hidden for ever," Liam said.

"I'm building a new stable beside the house. Have security lights and alarms on it. Major Simms is training a guard dog for me. Two, I hope. There's nothing like a couple of tough dogs to protect you."

Liam loved secrets. They gave him power, knowledge he kept to himself, that none of the rest of the family had. Some he shared with Romana, who was good at inventing new ideas, and who never spoke about them until she was sure they would work.

"When are you going to tell Noah?"

"When the new stable's ready. He knows something's up, but not what. I like secrets too. He'll love her."

"Is she very valuable?"

"Worth a king's ransom," Roy said. "She's heavily insured. With luck I'll have several foals from her, and they'll help keep the farm running. Insurance money wouldn't make up for that. It pays for the loss of the mare, not future foals."

"When does she have another foal?" he asked.

"Early next year. Mares go to the stud farm before the foals are born and meet the stallion soon afterwards. She stayed longer than most as I hadn't built this yet."

"How did you do it without Noah knowing?"

"In the evenings and at weekends. He doesn't come Sundays. I got up extra early. It's lovely at five in the morning. No one about and everything fresh. You can hear the grass growing."

He took a deep breath of air, almost as if he were drinking it.

"Nothing like country air. No smell of petrol and diesel fumes. You can taste the air in the towns. It tastes bad. Noah doesn't come till eight, as we've only Susie to milk. You can do a lot in three hours."

There were secrets everywhere, not only in his own home, Liam thought.

Back in the farmyard he went to look at his new acquisitions. Excitement overcame him. He was thirteen, he was grown up and he had a pig of his own. Two pigs. He had only spent fifteen out of his sixty pounds, and maybe if there were space somewhere on Roy's farm he could buy another. Then he'd have two sows. Perhaps he'd get stud fees for the little boar.

"I've still got forty-five pounds," Liam said to Roy, as they sat drinking Noah's stewed tea. Liam added three spoonfuls of sugar in an effort to make it more drinkable. Noah seemed to divide the day up into a number of breaks

34

for food, not always at times when everyone else ate. "Makes you fair starved, working out of doors," he would explain. "Need to keep our strength up. Hard work, not like sitting at a desk."

"Start a bank account, boy," he said. "Pigs cost money to feed. Can't expect Roy to pay your bills. Used to collect the leftovers from the schools after their dinners and make them into swill. EC won't let us do that now. Swill saved money. Have to buy pig pellets now. Got all the vitamins and minerals they need as well as nourishment, and it's all packed and germ free."

He snorted suddenly, and Liam stared at him alarmed, until he realised that the old man was laughing.

"Everything will be so hygienic that when we do meet a germ we'll all turn up our toes and die because we've no resistance to it," he said. "The Eskimos died of the white man's cold when we took it out there. Never met it before."

He spread butter lavishly on a thick slice of bread and cut himself a hunk of cheese.

"I used to work in a lab once, looking after the animals. They bred cats for experiments;

not nasty ones, mind, but they were testing out different foods to see which was best for them."

He paused to swallow an immense gulp of tea and chew hard at his enormous sandwich.

"Bred them in sterile surroundings. No germs anywhere. Then when we knew what was the best food, they were allowed into the real world, out of their specially made room. They were all dead within three months from germs that they'd never met before and had no immunity against. You can be too clean, young Liam."

"They knew nothing about our modern ways and medicines a couple of centuries ago, yet people still survived," Roy said. "Or none of us would be here."

"Dad often wonders how doctors would get on if they had to operate in the sort of places he does," Liam said. "Fields and barns and cow byres. Mostly the animals survive and the operation wounds don't even go septic."

"That may be due to antibiotics though." Roy took the end of the loaf, daubed it with mustard pickle and then spread it with slices of ham. "Eat, boy. Put some flesh on those bones of yours. Skinny as that new sheepdog of mine.

Haven't found out yet how to put weight on her."

Pintsize, Bran called him, teasing him mercilessly at times. Who wants to put weight on, Liam wondered. It never seems to come off and you can't eat everything you want to eat. Georgie had been on a diet for the past six months, as she had gained over twelve kilos when she was unable to walk or exercise hard. All of them seemed to suffer with Georgie, and Grandma had stopped making cakes and scones and pies and pasties and fed them all on salads. But they were back on their more usual diet now.

Liam looked out of the window, watching Greg playing with one of his kittens. The tiny animal was ginger, like his father, and patted at the big cat's face, and then chased his waving tail. Greg looked as if he were deliberately enticing the baby to jump on it.

"Teaching him to mouse," Roy said.

There were always new animals on a farm. Old Jack, the sheepdog, was now nearly ten years old and beginning to stiffen. Soon he'd be retired, a live-in-the-house and sleep-by-the-fire dog.

"The new pup has a lot to learn," Roy said. The young collie was nearly a year old, bought from another farmer when Roy realised that Jack's days were numbered. Jack was a big heavy dog but little Pip was smaller, lightly built, coal-black, with white paws and a white patch on one side of her face, with a smooth coat and bright eyes and prick ears that never stopped listening. She lay in the yard, watching Greg and the kitten, knowing that she must not chase them.

Roy stretched, easing his aching muscles.

"Pip has to learn to herd sheep and not chase them. To bring the cattle in. To herd the pigs for me. She's starting on the ducks. Does it for fun, and she isn't chasing, which is a good sign. Have to watch her though. One mistake with a dog and you have a lifetime's problem. Reason why so many family dogs go wrong."

"Like Khan, when Jed kept telling him to switch on the light or shut the door, and he got sick of it, so we had to send Jed away for a while," Liam said, with vivid memories of those days when Georgie couldn't move from her bed, and everyone was miserable. Her room had been specially adapted so that the dog could do all kinds of things for her. The wall switch for the light had been replaced by a toggle on a cord that Khan could tug with his mouth.

"Lost a lot more animals through illness and infection when I were a lad," Noah said. Sometimes Liam wondered if the old man knew much about the present. The past seemed more important to him, and he rarely seemed to listen properly to the conversations going on around him. This made life confusing at times, as he came back to subjects everyone else thought had been exhausted or went off on an entirely different track.

"I sometimes feel I'm on the M1 and Noah is tootling up a country lane, and we're miles apart," Roy had once said. "I'm discussing how much feed to give the boar and he's gone way back to his childhood and honeysuckle in the lanes when he was a boy."

Noah was expanding now on a theme that Liam had heard before.

"Maybe there's something to be said for modern ways, but I still think you can go too far." Both Roy and Liam waited for him to continue, but instead he rammed his cap on his wiry hair and walked out of the room.

"How much will it cost me to feed Porgy and

Bess?" Liam asked, the worry surfacing.

"I'll keep accounts, and let you know. Give you a bill each week. Won't overdo it, I promise."

Cycling home, Liam thought about his pigs and his new responsibilities.

"A journey always starts with one step," Noah said as he left. "The road twists and turns and you can't see round the corner. Life's like that, boy."

No use making plans, Georgie always said. She'd once intended to be one of the best show-jumpers in Britain, but her accident meant that could never happen. They'd said she'd never walk again, but she was walking, though with a slight limp, and she was riding, though she never would ride in top competitions.

"A year of being in a wheelchair, unable to walk or run, gives you a different attitude to life," she said. "You have to fight to win." Liam was beginning to understand her view-point. Everyone laughed at his passion for pigs. He'd show them. He might be the youngest of them all and way behind them in years but one day he'd do better than any of them. Mean-while he had a lot to think about.

He'd need all his pocket money now for his

new acquisitions. No more casual buying of sweets and cassettes. A thin rain began, and he pedalled harder, wanting to get home and go up to his room and work out some sums. Maybe being thirteen did mean a different world. He had never thought before of the money Roy had to pay out: for pig feed, for vet bills, for repairs to the farm machinery, for his own food and clothes and Noah's wages.

He'd have to find a way of making more money each week. His pocket money wasn't nearly enough.

Money doesn't grow on trees. How often had Grandma Bridie said that.

And how he wished it did.

CHAPTER 4

Liam was not sure whether the House of Secrets bred secrets, or created them, or induced its inhabitants to keep them. He did not want anyone to know he now owned pigs. Not that it mattered. No one would object though they might laugh at him. It would be kind laughter, but he hated people thinking his affairs funny. Also having his own life was part of being grown up. It was nothing to do with anyone else.

All the same, he worried. Suppose things went wrong? Maybe Roy would find it a nuisance to have someone else's pigs to care for. Maybe he would be unable to go there often enough. He'd be expected to help with the chores. Maybe he couldn't afford the pig food.

Later, when they were a little older, they'd be put out to forage for their own food with Roy's pigs. Or would they? He hadn't asked nearly enough questions, mainly because he hadn't realised there were questions to ask.

He arrived home at surgery time. There seemed to be an unusual number of dogs tonight, some of them barking, and from the surgery came a high-pitched squealing. Lois saw him cycle into the yard and came to the door and called him.

"Liam, can you come and sit by the phone and answer for me? It's like Paddy's market tonight."

Liam propped his bike against the wall. He was aware of Troy's forlorn face watching him through the kitchen window opposite, but there was no time for her as the phone was already ringing.

"Longmoor Farm. Possible bracken poisoning." He wrote it down. "My father will be with you as soon as surgery is over," he said, hoping that was true. He raised an eyebrow and Lois paused in dealing with a client trying to control a dancing terrier and take money from her bag. She looked at the note and nodded.

There was a welcome pause, as the last comers settled, and nobody else came in. The squeals began again, redoubling in intensity.

"What on earth's making that noise?" Liam thought it sounded like a pig.

"Dave Garrod's terrier. She loathes having her claws cut. She's been sedated but it still takes three people to hang on to her, and one to snip. Never seen anything like it."

Liam thought of Troy who sat sedately and lifted each paw in turn to have her claws cut.

"Are there many like that?" he asked. He rarely helped in surgery. Bran had always done that. He would have to stand in at times, he realised. Perhaps this too was what being thirteen instead of twelve was all about. He'd evaded a lot of little chores because he was the baby in the family. Nobody expected him to be able to do them. Time they realised he was grown up.

"Not many," Lois said, answering a question Liam had forgotten he had asked. "Seelie's a rescue. Dave didn't get her till she was three years old. He's done a great job. She looked as if she had never been groomed in her life. Full of fleas and ticks and a very mucky coat."

Lois paused to take details from a woman holding a Siamese kitten under her arm. The kitten looked at Liam out of blue eyes that squinted. Liam put out a finger and tickled her cheek and she purred, squeezing her eyes shut and opening them again. Her owner laughed.

"She can take any amount of that," she said, as she went to sit down. The kitten mewed noisily, annoyed because the fussing was over.

Lois sighed.

"Surgery seems to have been going on for ever," she said.

Liam glanced at the record book. There were more than twenty names in it. They had been busy. The squeals had stopped. The surgery door opened and the Jack Russell bitch flew out, bracing herself to get to the door and race through it before anyone could do anything else awful to her.

"I'll put her in the car, then come back and pay," her owner said, holding on desperately and galloping out at the end of the lead. He was a small square man, as wide as he was high, with a bright red face, that Liam thought was probably due to embarrassment. They vanished out of the door. Lois asked the next owner to go in for treatment.

"She's impossible," Dave Garrod said, when he came back to pay. "Happens every time. I keep hoping she'll grow out of it, but she never has."

The Siamese kitten mewed suddenly.

"It's her second injection," her owner said. "She hated the first." She got up to go into the surgery as Dave Garrod paid and went out.

"Dave's had a tough time with her," said Lois. "She was rescued by the RSPCA from a man who drank too much and used to kick and hit her. She was terrified of people, of loud noises, and of bottles. We think he threw them at her. It took a long time to get her trust. Claw cutting needs to be started when they're babies. Then they take it as part of life."

The waiting-room door opened again, and a woman came in, holding a curly-coated struggling creature under one arm.

Liam glanced at the animal, thinking it a strange-looking dog and then realised it was a lamb.

"A latecomer," the woman said. "Born to a ewe that was supposed not to have another lamb. She had her own ideas and escaped into the ram's field. She had problems giving birth and my husband had to help her, but managed somehow to break its leg."

"Always something. That's not one I've heard before," Lois said. "It would be easy though if you aren't experienced and there's a problem birth."

The little creature looked odd when they came back, its hind leg in plaster.

"Bring it back to have it changed as it grows, or we'll have real problems," Josh Murray said, from the surgery door.

"This is going to be a very expensive lamb," the owner said with a sigh, handing over a number of notes which Lois put in the till. Liam looked at them in dismay. Suppose something like that happened to Porgy or Bess. Could he afford to have treatment for them?

Surgery ended at last and Josh Murray came out to look at the appointments book, unbuttoning his white coat as he walked over to them. He examined the entries carefully.

"Better go over to Longmoor Farm. Harry doesn't fuss over nothing. Your birthday tea will have to wait, Liam. Want to come?"

"Please." There was nothing else to do. "Can Troy come? She's been alone all afternoon. I went over to Roy's. He needed some help."

"Be quick then."

Lois was clearing up. Romana appeared, taking a bucket and mop into the surgery to swab everything down ready for morning. Troy, released into the yard, raced round it at top speed, delighted to be free, and then, seeing the Land Rover open, leaped in and looked at Liam and his father as if defying them to evict her.

"Not like Longmoor Farm to have bracken poisoning," Liam's father said, negotiating a blind bend very carefully. "Harry Lake's a very careful man. There won't be any poisonous plants anywhere on his land. Can't see how they got it. Did he say what animals?"

"Just that he thought he had a case of bracken poisoning," Liam said.

They turned into a narrow lane that twisted up a hill and seemed to go on for ever. At last they came to the farm. Liam climbed out to open the gate into the yard, checking carefully to make sure that there were no animals free. There were reddish-brown chickens and a large handsome cock scratching in the dust at the far side of the yard outside a barn piled high with hay, but no sign of any other creatures.

Two tabby cats sat on either side of the gate, perched on the posts, looking like statues. They watched with interest and one of them, seeing Troy in the Land Rover window, spat noisily and sped into the barn.

Yellow roses climbed up the farmhouse wall on one side of the studded oak door. On the other side a trained apricot tree promised a welcome harvest in a few weeks' time.

"My old hunter," Harry Lake said, appearing like a genie from the barn. "Some idiot left a gate open and he got out. Been feeding up on the hill there. I'd like to burn the bracken off, but it's not my hill. Pestilential stuff. If the land were properly managed . . ."

A horned billy-goat, tethered by the far side of the barn, stopped grazing and glared at them out of yellow eyes. Satan's beasts, Noah called them. He hated goats. Liam quite liked them so long as they showed no sign of butting him. Troy, sitting in front of the steering wheel in the Land Rover, looked out at them happily.

Leo, the hunter, was a massive horse, perhaps with some shire in him, Liam thought. His eyes were dull and his coat had lost its sheen. He stood, head hanging, without much interest in any of them.

"Couldn't account for it," Harry said, patting the strong neck. "He's getting old, poor fellow. Only use him for hacking about the lanes. I never did hunt. Bought him from a man who was going to shoot him because he was past it." Leo did not even turn his head. His body twitched as if he were shaking off flies, but there were none on his coat. "I'd forgotten that afternoon till my wife reminded me when we were racking our brains as to what could be wrong with him. Had a calf with the same symptoms twenty years ago. Another gate left open. That one died."

Josh Murray nodded thoughtfully. That had been before his time.

"He was free for some hours before we found him." Harry caressed the soft muzzle. "He doesn't even seem to notice me. He's usually so responsive and loves us making a fuss. Won't even touch an apple and he adores those."

"I hope we've got it soon enough," Josh Murray said. He looked into the horse's eyes, checked his ears, and felt all over his body. "What sort of symptoms?"

"Lack-lustre all the time. Doesn't want to eat and his walking's unsteady."

"The injections might cure it. Depends on how far gone he is." Leo stood impassively, as if unaware of their presence or even of the syringe as the needle sank in.

"None of the others got out?" Josh asked.

"No. He was in the far field on his own. The mare's just foaled. Come and look at the baby. He's a charmer."

The tiny chestnut foal was feeding from the big mare. Their colours were so alike that he was almost invisible against her body. She nosed him, and looked at them over his back.

"Four white socks," Josh Murray said, and grinned.

"I don't believe that old nonsense. Proved it not to be true time and again," Harry said, his voice testy.

"What old nonsense?" Liam asked, wondering what on earth they were talking about. The foal had four white legs. His mother only had two. The other two were chestnut right down to her hooves.

"One white sock, try it.
Two white socks, buy it.
Three white socks, look well about it.
Four white socks, you're best without it."

Josh declaimed it like a litany and Harry snorted.

It was the kind of rhyme that Noah liked. Liam decided to ask the old man if he knew it next time he went to see Porgy and Bess.

"Cup of tea?" Harry asked.

"It's Liam's birthday. They'll be waiting for us at home. Grandma enjoys a celebration," Josh said. "Another time. I'll look in tomorrow. With luck, he'll recover. Let's hope he stays on his legs. Be a problem if he falls."

"I wouldn't mind ramblers if they'd behave, and shut gates and not leave polythene about. Kill more animals that way than by disease. Makes farming harder than need be and it's tough already." Harry sighed deeply and walked over to open the gate for them.

Grandma Bridie had laid their meal in the dining room, which they only used on state occasions. The kitchen was much more convenient and more friendly, Liam thought. The dining room was a formal room. The dogs were not usually allowed there, but Troy tonight was part of the family, and came in to drop down at Liam's feet and put her nose on his shoe and sighed deeply.

Liam suddenly wondered if she thought Bran

had gone away for ever. He would be home, but only briefly. When he came, Liam knew he wouldn't have a dog at all. And then Bran would go again and Troy would take days to get over his loss.

It was lonely without Bran and his sisters – who had all left home now – even though they had so often quarrelled, and Bran teased him. Liam had never had a birthday on his own before. He didn't want a party. He was too old for that, and none of the boys at school shared any of his interests. His parents were there, and Lois and Romana.

He bent down and stroked Troy, wishing that she would attach herself to him and forget his brother.

The table was laid with the birthday cloth, only used on such occasions. It was elaborately embroidered. It had been given them, when they moved to the House of Secrets, by Romana, who made the most wonderful patterned clothes and covers. There were puppies and kittens, lambs and butterflies, foals and dainty deer fawns. Every time that Liam looked at it, he found a new animal to marvel at. It was much too good for everyday use.

There were two parcels by his plate. In the

centre of the table was a huge cake, shaped like a pig, with thirteen candles glowing on it. His birthday cards were on the mantelpiece. He remembered Noah's cake and went out to get it from his cycle bag.

As he came in everyone began to sing.

"Happy birthday to you, happy birthday to you, happy birthday, dear Liam, happy birthday to you."

Troy, startled, sat up and barked.

Everyone laughed and she lay down again and put her nose on her paws, unable to understand what had been funny.

"Happy birthday to you. Happy, happy, happy," shouted Jed from the kitchen and began to miaow so that Troy barked at him.

"I sometimes wonder why we keep him," Liam's mother Sally said, laughing, as she poured her special fruit punch into the glasses on the table and added slices of lemon and sprigs of mint.

Grandma took an apple, cut it into quarters and went out with it to give it to the mynah bird to keep him quiet. With luck it would last him all through the meal, as he adored fruit.

The room seemed full in spite of the fact that the twins and Jenna were missing. Lois and

Romana had both changed out of their worka-day clothes.

Grandma had cooked a big ham which Josh Murray sliced carefully, while his wife passed him the plates. Potato and rice salads, little bowls of pickled onions and pickled beetroot, and cucumbers and tomatoes diced together in Liam's favourite mayonnaise that no one else knew how to make, as Grandma treasured the recipe. Sausage rolls and pastries filled with chicken cooked in wine sauce. Meringues and cream. There looked enough for an army, Liam thought. His meal with Roy had not spoiled his appetite.

"Not going to open your parcels?" his mother asked. "We're all dying of curiosity, even if you aren't."

The first was heavy. It was wrapped in brightly coloured paper, decorated with bal-loons and teddy bears. Anyone would think I was a baby still, Liam thought resentfully, hoping the contents were better suited to his years.

A paperweight. The bronze pig had a quiz-zical expression, as if it were laughing. The card with it, also showing a large pig rooting thoughtfully in grass studded with buttercups, had a message printed in capitals.

"Thirteen. Cor! Babies do grow up, it seems. Welcome to the real world. You're a big boy now. Mind you take care of Troy for me. Love from your horrible big brother, Bran."

Liam grinned, seeing Bran as plainly as if he were in the room, with his shock of hair that always needed cutting and his broad smile and his absurd sense of humour. It was good to know he hadn't forgotten.

The other parcel intrigued him. He felt through the gold wrapping paper, wondering if he could guess what it was. A box of some kind? Everyone was watching him.

It was a box. More like a casket and it was very old. A small pig sat on the lid, its head on one side. The ornamental hinges were dark with age and the clasp had been mended. He opened the lid and caught his breath. The soft tinkling tune was familiar and yet it was strange, the notes falling on his ears like a half-forgotten memory.

And then Romana was singing, her voice startling them all into silence.

"Orpheus with his lute made trees,
And the mountain tops that freeze
Bow themselves as he did sing . . ."

Liam was suddenly transported by the sounds from the box and Romana's clear voice, keeping them all spellbound.

The song ended and Liam came back to reality.

"It's very old," Romana said. "I found it at the back of one of those dark little shops where there are all sorts of hidden treasures that other people haven't valued or have been forced to sell. I thought you'd like to have something unique. I could never have let anyone else have it, had it been mine."

"Don't you want to keep it?" Liam asked, caressing the shining wood with his fingers.

"I know you love music," Romana said. "I didn't buy it for myself. I bought it to give as a present, but I had to find someone who would value it as much as I do."

That night, just before he fell asleep, Liam listened to an exchange of greetings between two calling owls and thought of badgers in the wood, hunting for food, going about their own business. In their sty Porgy and Bess would be sleeping, close together.

It had, after all, been a wonderful day, a day to remember for the rest of his life. Grandma had kissed him goodnight, and hugged him, as he went up to bed.

"I often think life is like an unwritten book," she said. "You never know what's going to happen when you turn the page, but a lot of what happens is entirely up to you. Don't waste it."

A voice followed him up the stairs. Romana's voice, but she had long gone home.

"Charlie is my darling, my darling, my darling,
  Charlie is my darling,
  The young cavalier."

The song ended with the sound of two cats fighting, a loud cough and a woeful cry.

"Jed's lonely. Poor Jed. Don't waste it."

The voice was cut off suddenly as Grandma covered the mynah for the night.

Liam turned over and grinned in the darkness. He was glad that he wasn't yet as old as the twins and Jenna. He loved the House of Secrets and wished that he could live there for ever and never grow up and never have to leave it.

CHAPTER 5

Liam woke to a grey morning with clouds chasing across the sky. The wind was a noise in the trees, a waving in the bushes, an irritation to the animals. The horses, out in the paddock eating the summer grass, were skittish, rolling and romping, bucking and racing, as if chased by demons. They hated the wind under their tails.

July was giving way to August with a day that would soon be dominated by a roaring gale. The holidays had begun. Seven free weeks before he was trapped again by time, chasing to keep up with the relentless clock. Seven weeks to enjoy his pigs. He planned to spend most of his time with Roy and Noah. No one would mind. He would ask each morning if they needed him to help at all at home.

Troy was sitting by his bed, looking at him with large, reproachful brown eyes. Bran was always up at half-past six, out with her, playing with her, training her, and she missed the morning routine. She had suffered from not being able to go out and run off her energy for long enough.

She now knew that Liam was the source of her food and her walks, and he would have to be taught that he could not lie in bed when she needed to go out. She pawed at him impatiently.

He looked at his watch.

Seven o'clock. He never got up till seven-thirty, even though on school days that meant a wild scramble to get everything done before he caught the bus. He suddenly realised why Bran was always up so early. Troy was now his and he would have to exercise her before breakfast. He would have to be up earlier on schooldays. Part of his money must go on buying an alarm clock. Grandma refused to waken any of them.

"Your fault if you're late, not mine," she

said. "The sooner you learn that, the better. Nobody comes and wakes me up. It's entirely up to me. My job is to get breakfast. Not to run around as if you were all babies."

He was no longer the youngest in the family. He was the only one in the family. No one else would exercise Troy. That, his father had said firmly, was Liam's responsibility, as was grooming her, and feeding her. If he forgot, Troy would go and live with Romana and only come back when Bran was home.

He needed to work out a routine so that he could call in and see to the pigs after school, and make sure all was well with them. Then there was homework and there'd be more of it next term. He was going up a class, into the third form. He suddenly felt overwhelmed. It had been exciting to think of himself as a pig owner, but he had not thought hard enough about all the chores that went with that.

Troy barked at him impatiently. She wanted to be out of doors, running in the paddock, chasing after shadows. There was a tickle in her paws that told her she must race and riot, with the wind in her fur and excitement building.

Lois's mare had a new foal and she wanted to find out about him, and see if he would race against her.

Liam washed and dressed, pulling on a jersey as the wind was cool. Outside in the yard Troy raced to the paddock gate and circled wildly, unable to stand still for a second. Bran would have made her, would have told her to sit and wait until the gate was open but Liam had not yet learned that dogs mustn't always have their own way. That made them impossible to live with as they could take over leading the family pack and everyone would have to do as the dog chose, not as they wanted.

She butted against him before the gate was halfway open, eager to reach freedom. He fell, banging his shoulder against the gatepost, and was angry with her, shouting at her.

"You stupid dog. Why did you do that?"

He felt hurt and angry. She never behaved like that with Bran. Why couldn't she behave with him? Bran had trained her, hadn't he?

Troy ran down the field and stood and looked at him, telling him that she was not coming near unless he behaved himself.

The horses in the next paddock leaned their heads over the rail fence, watching the dog as she flew over the grass, running at top speed, ecstatic with happiness and freedom. Liam let her run. She would use more energy this way than he could work off if he took her for a walk. Also he was not at all sure he would enjoy the walk as she had begun to pull on the lead as if she were a puppy again.

He supposed she was missing Bran and playing up because of it. Maybe when they went out she thought that she might find him. Life must be very odd for dogs, Liam thought, watching her. There was no way he could tell her Bran wasn't gone for ever, though he'd only be home for short periods now.

Liam himself would go away one day though that day was five years in the future. Troy would be eleven years old then. His pigs would be five years old. What would happen in those five years? Life stretched ahead of him, a total mystery.

Troy picked up the broken branch of a tree, an absurd trophy, which looked far too heavy to carry. She teased it until it was balanced in her jaws and then swaggered across the field carrying it.

It was a showing-off game of her own that she played for Bran. It was fun but she had

never before played it for Liam and he felt that
he had achieved some understanding with her.
He left the gate slightly ajar. It was heavy and
needed lifting to latch. There was nothing in
this paddock. The horses would be put there
tomorrow, leaving the other paddock free.

The rising wind sang in the branches of the
trees beside the lake. The swans swam, their
five grey cygnets in line behind them and a
moorhen rushed busily through the reeds.
There were already berries on the rowan trees.

Noah said that rowans protected people from
witchcraft. He always grew one in his own
garden, and had insisted that Roy planted a
number of the handsome trees around the yard
to protect the animals.

Roy didn't believe in witches or in spells,
but only in good husbandry and care, but he
gave the old man his way. No harm in the
trees, and the berries brought birds to feast.
Roy enjoyed the birds. He also enjoyed Noah's
stories, and so did Liam, although he thought
they were often nonsense.

A magpie flirted across the field, its tail
frisking. Noah said you had to salute them
when you only saw one, or it brought bad luck.
Liam pretended to push his hair out of his

eyes, lifting his hand shamefacedly, thinking how silly it was, yet half afraid that something bad would happen if he didn't acknowledge the bird.

Its mate flew out of a tree and perched beside it.

One for sorrow.

Two for joy.

So that was all right. He stood watching the bright feathers, blue-black in the faint sun that escaped between the clouds. They were shabby after rearing their families.

Troy was still struggling to get her branch out of the paddock and into the yard.

She ran at the gate and the branch jammed. There was no way she could carry it through. She backed off, eyed the gap and tried again, charging with such force that she was rocked back on her paws as she met the edges of the gate and the gatepost and again she was foiled. She barked at the gate, annoyed by its lack of co-operation.

Liam watched her, entertained, wondering if she would ever work out how to go through the gap. He wondered also if he were being unkind and ought to open it wider, but he was curious to see if she could work out the problem.

She tried twice more and then sat. She had no intention of letting go of her treasure. She loved branches, not sticks, and the bigger the better. She often tried to drag some that were almost as big as she was.

She laid her find on the ground, and looked thoughtfully at the gate. She lined the branch so that it was level with the gap, and turned it, so that it lay straight and not at an angle to the opening.

She walked through the gate, turned round, picked up the unwieldy object and dragged it through, backing away. With a triumphant flirt of her tail she picked it up again and swaggered across to the kitchen door, waiting to be let in.

"You can't take that in," Liam said. He tried to take it from her, but she held it firmly, tugging at it, wanting to retain it. He left it with her and walked into the kitchen, shutting the door behind him.

Troy looked at the closed door. It was time for her breakfast. She was not sure which she wanted most. The branch or the food, but food won. She dropped her prize and barked.

Liam opened the door and she ran in.

"That'll learn yer," said Jed, in a voice that Liam had never heard before. He grinned, wondering as he always did if the bird actually knew what it was saying and made sense, or if it was just luck that some of the things he repeated fitted the moment.

"Jed's lonely. Where's Bran? Where's Georgie? Where's Jenna?"

"It is lonely without them," Liam said, putting Troy's dish down on the floor. She was impatient to have it, dancing again, twisting and turning, unable to be still.

"You need to make her sit still for her food. Bran always does," Grandma said, unaware that she could have said nothing more likely to make Liam cross.

"I hate being the youngest." Liam sat down and attacked his plate of bacon and bread dipped in egg and fried. "The others have all the fun and do everything better than I do."

"They didn't at your age. Besides, you have something they have never had." Grandma spread a slice of toast with marmalade, and bit into it. Troy, who took about two minutes to bolt her food, came to sit at her side, and eyed the plate with longing.

"What's that?" Liam couldn't imagine anything that was unique to him.

"Jenna was an only child for a very few years

that she won't remember and then the twins came and then you. The twins always had you and Jenna. None of them has ever had the privilege of being the only one for five years, without any of the others around."

"It just means I have to do all the jobs and there's no one else to share them." Liam was determined to be contrary. The wind was irritating and he wished the noise would stop. A sudden gust blew against the door and windows and then the rain rattled down, drumming on the paving stones in the yard. The keening at the corners always reminded him of children crying, and when he was younger the noise had worried him immensely.

"I wanted to go over to Roy. I'll get soaked if I cycle," Liam said. Everything was going wrong with the day.

"Your dad's going past the farm. If he drops you there, I'll fetch you," Grandma said. That meant waiting until after surgery had ended. Liam took the comb and began to groom Troy, astounded by the amount of fur that came out.

"She's moulting," Josh Murray said, coming into the room. "I had a client once who brought her new pup to the surgery, desperately worried because it was losing its fur." He laughed and took two slices of toast from the rack that was keeping warm on top of the Aga. "She'd never had a dog before and didn't know they shed their coats when the weather changes. She had visions of walking round the town with a bald animal."

"There ought to be warnings sold with pups," Grandma said briskly, as she tidied away her plate and mug. "No end of dogs seem to come into the Rescue Centre because the owners can't stand fur all over the place, and want a nice clean tidy house."

Grandma helped at the Centre three times a week, walking the dogs that were waiting for new owners. She was always tempted to bring them all home, and was never very happy on those days.

"There was a gorgeous little bitch brought in last week," she said as Liam's mother raced into the room, and stood, as if poised to fly away. "I'd have loved to bring her home with me."

"I don't know what happens in the mornings," Sally Murray said crossly, pouring coffee into a mug. "I never seem able to get up at the time I plan. The minutes just race by." She was out of the room and into her car almost before she had had time to finish drinking. Liam was reminded of Georgie, who was also always late for everything and never seemed able to understand how clocks worked.

His father picked up the clean white coat that lay on the windowsill ready for him.

"Could I beg a lift to Roy's?" Liam asked, afraid his father would say no.

"Sure. I need to go the second surgery ends. There's a mare at Stokes Farm that jumped wire and has a gash on her leg."

Liam dried up the dishes for Grandma who started to ask, teasingly, if he felt ill. She changed her mind. Maybe having the others away would make him more thoughtful. She sat to make out her shopping list. Liam stared out at the rain, now lashing down. He'd need his oilskins.

By the time he had found them, hidden away in a corner of a cupboard in Bran's room, his father was waiting. He raced downstairs, without a backward glance at Troy, who looked mournfully after him. Liam wasn't yet used to taking her around with him as Bran had.

Roy and Noah were both busy at the little sty where Liam's two pigs were housed.

"Glad you've come," Roy said. "Little one's

causing us problems. Need your dad. I was just going to ring him."

"Reckon it's just the change of routine, from Mum to bottle," Noah said, a worried look on his face. "Could be baby pig disease." That was bad.

Liam looked at him in dismay. It sounded as if she might die after all. Roy had warned him. He hadn't paid anything for her, but even so, he couldn't bear the thought of losing her.

Porgy, the little Berkshire pig, was rooting in a corner of the sty. His bright eyes considered Liam and he came and snorted at him, sounding as if he were asking a question. The grunts continued happily and Liam scratched his small damp snout.

Bess lay in the corner, her eyes dull, and didn't even turn her head when Liam knelt beside her.

He hadn't considered a possible early death. Sadly, he began to realise there was far more to the care of any animal than he had imagined. It was one thing to dream of keeping pigs. Quite another to own the real animal.

CHAPTER 6

"Better get your dad," Roy said. "Just to check there's nothing very serious and catching wrong with her. Can't risk the other pigs. Maybe we ought to move Porgy."

"Don't tell my dad she's mine."

"Why ever not?"

"They'd laugh at me." Liam hated people laughing at him and the family did tease him about his pig obsession.

Bran had found a cartoon of people sitting in a pigsty with the pigs bringing them their food, and had it framed. On the same day he had found a cartoon for his father, of a man stuffing a barn to the top with bills, all labelled VET BILL. This now hung in the waiting room and caused a lot of amusement.

"No need for your dad to know," Roy said. "I don't see why you worry, though. Nothing wrong with pigs. I'm pretty crazy about them too. Had dreams once of having pigs trained to find truffles and making me a fortune, or teaching them circus tricks and getting on the telly."

"Are there truffles in England?"

"Used to be, in the South. Don't know if there still are. Not likely to be any round here. Mostly they grow in France, I believe. Probably use dogs now. There's nothing like a dog's nose for finding smells."

"Dad's out, but he could call in on his way back if they catch him at Stokes Farm. One of the mares has jumped wire."

"I'll ring," Noah said, appearing suddenly, as he often did, from behind the sty. He vanished as abruptly as he had arrived.

"He always reminds me of a pantomime magician," Liam said. "Likely some time to arrive in a puff of smoke. I never hear him coming."

" Soft-soled shoes. I don't know how he does it though with his arthritis. It's bad again," Roy said. "He doesn't get any younger. Don't let on though. The time's going to come . . ." Roy had a habit of not finishing sentences, usually turning away to do something else. He seemed to live life at a gallop, never in one place for more than a few seconds.

"They had louts chasing the horses at Stokes Farm," he added, remembering what Liam had said. "Pigfeed lorry driver told me."

The lorry driver carried the news from farm to farm. Nothing could be kept secret for very long. Once the Arab mare came into the stable building in the yard, everyone would know about Roy's latest acquisition.

Roy was burrowing in a cupboard. He reappeared holding a large syringe without a needle. "I'll try giving that little one some milk through this." He sighed. "We all have trouble. I had lads round here last week, throwing stones at the pigs in the big paddock. I'd have liked to set Solomon on them."

Solomon was a big and irritable gander that guarded the farm. Noah reckoned geese were more useful than dogs as protectors. Those who were unwelcome beat a speedy retreat as Solomon half-flew, half-ran at them, wings outstretched, presenting a truly fearsome sight.

"What did you do?"

Roy was dripping milk from the syringe into Bess's mouth. She didn't even try to swallow. It trickled down her chin. He opened her mouth and put the syringe inside, and then stroked her throat.

Roy laughed, remembering.

"Nothing. Noah had been out shooting rabbits and came round the corner with his gun. He had no idea that the boys were there. They didn't half make off fast when they saw him. Don't think they'll be back in a hurry. The gun wasn't loaded, but they didn't know that."

Liam followed Roy round the farm, feeling forlorn. The five Chinese geese waddled after them, eternally curious. They were small and sleek and grey in colour, very unlike the big white geese and gander. Wherever Roy or Noah went, the delicate little creatures seemed to dog their footsteps. They reminded Liam of inquisitive old ladies, eager to see everything that went on, yet probably not understanding it all. Solomon, the gander, was penned by day but he was free to wander at night, in spite of the risk of foxes. Noah was sure the fox would come off worst. Solomon had a temper and fought stray dogs if they came on to the property, backing up the farm dogs, much to the men's amusement. Any intruder so tackled kept clear. Few people stopped to argue with the gander who could put on a remarkable turn of speed. He was likely to bite when he caught up with the person. He weighed a considerable amount and was no easy creature to tangle with. He was the only farm creature that frightened Liam.

They turned the corner of the yard. An old wagon, half repaired and half painted, stood in the corner against the barn.

"What's that for?"

"That's another item for the farm museum. Wonderful old thing, isn't it? It was at Stoke Farm. Must have been there for years. They were getting rid of it. Going to turn their barn into a farm shop. Harry intended to chop it up for firewood, but luckily I saw it and he let me have it for a tenner. A real bargain."

He stroked one of the huge spokes lovingly. The cart was an odd-looking object, the four wheels as high as the top of the slatted side-pieces. One end was open for loading. The other was made of a piece of solid wood.

Liam had never seen anything like it.

Roy pushed it, easing it a few yards, rolling on soundlessly.

"Moves sweetly," he said. "Noah and I spent hours doing it up and painting it. Maybe we could use it to give rides to children. Or enter it as a showpiece at the County Fair."

There were so many things you could do if you thought about them, Liam decided, as he padded behind Roy towards the big paddock where Colossus lived. On the far side of the grass was a small lake that the pigs loved, wallowing at the edge of it.

Colossus was Roy's prize boar. He was an enormous animal, with a great liking for humans and the temperament of an amiable dog. Colossus trying to rub himself against anyone was very likely to land that person on the ground, so that Liam spent a great deal of his time avoiding the huge animal.

That triggered Colossus to try even harder to make contact.

At first sight there was nothing to be seen but the ducks, some swimming on the pond, some rooting around the edges. Roy had left the tractor in the field, ready for use, and three hens sat happily on its bonnet, while two more were in the trailer. Giant trees on the far side of the water cast shadows across the ground, their leaves shivering in the wind. There were pigs beneath them, rooting for food, but none was big enough to be Colossus. Muddy hillocks bordered the water.

"Now where's that boar gone?" Roy asked, scratching his head. He resettled his cap. "He can't have got out."

A brown hen appeared from behind the tractor, clucking worriedly to the eight yellow chicks that sped after her, as if afraid they were all going to be lost.

"Well, well," said Roy. "So that's what she's been up to. Vanished a few weeks ago and we thought the fox had her. She must have been sitting on her eggs in Colossus's sty. Maybe he's in there."

The big sty was empty. There were traces of eggshells in the straw.

"She's as bad as the cats, that one," Roy said. "Never can find their kittens. Tucked away in the barn, or even once in the rafters and that caused problems. We heard them when she was away hunting and had to climb up and get them down before they all fell down."

"Would they have hurt themselves?" Liam asked.

"Could have done. Cats don't always land on

all four feet and these were babies that hadn't any practice at jumping from heights."

He was scanning the field as he spoke.

"No one could lose a boar the size of Colossus. He's massive. I hope he hasn't drowned himself."

"Couldn't he swim? Or float?"

"Dunno. Never have tried to see if my pigs could swim. There's an old tale that if they do fall in water they cut their throats with their hooves as they try to swim, but I reckon that's an old wives' tale. Sounds daft to me."

"Like if you hold up a guinea-pig by its tail its eyes drop out," Liam said.

"Not really. Guinea-pigs don't have tails. Pigs do have trotters. They could be sharp-edged."

Why call them trotters, Liam wondered. Not many of the pigs trotted, though maybe they did when they smelled food. Especially the little ones, who rushed and shoved and pushed and butted one another. A little surprisingly he found they reminded him of school at dinner time. Everyone jostling to be first at the counter where the food was put on to the plates, unless a teacher was there to call them all to order.

A massive lump suddenly reared itself from

the far side of the pond and lumbered towards them, scattering the ducks. Colossus, who was a Gloucester Old Spot, was normally pink with black splodges, but he appeared now to have covered himself in thick mud.

"No wonder we couldn't see him. Wallowing to keep cool," Roy said, hastily vaulting the gate and holding out a hand to help Liam over. "He'll want his tummy rubbed and he'll push against us and we'll both get covered in mud. Silly fellow, he's done himself out of a treat. Have to get Noah to turn the hose on him. He'll love that. Probably why he does get so mucky. So he can be cleaned up."

Colossus, deprived of his daily pleasure, chased after them, grunting loudly. He rubbed himself against the gate, his lop ears flapping over his eyes and big snout.

"I wish the lads had come this way," Roy said, as they headed back towards the farm-yard. "Colossus isn't exactly comforting when he charges and not many people know he only wants to be tickled." He laughed. "Saw a little lass there one day, taking a short cut. Colossus saw her too and decided to make friends. Never seen anyone run so fast. Noah and me couldn't stop laughing. Real cross she was when we showed her what he wanted. He rolled over and groaned in ecstasy as we rubbed him. She didn't think it a bit funny." He laughed again at the memory, and led Liam to the far side of the big yard.

"Got me another Tamworth," Roy said. "Come and look at her. Going to see what happens if I cross her with Colossus. Red pigs with black splodges, do you think? Her name's Matilda, if you please. Named by the children on the farm where she came from. They had a bull there that the kids had named too."

He stopped talking and laughed again. Roy seemed to find life more amusing than anyone he had ever met, Liam thought. They had once got lost when visiting another farm to buy some pigs. Instead of getting cross Roy had commented that this was a terrific adventure and think of all the things they'd have missed if they'd found the right road at once.

One of the things they would have missed was a tiny roadside stall selling the most luscious hot dogs that Liam had ever tasted. Another was a cottage where a beautiful Burmese cat played in the garden with her kittens. Roy had stopped the car to watch.

Maybe it was being with the pigs all the time

that made him find life so good. Roy's were all very happy animals, with characters of their own which they had a chance to develop, living free.

Liam suddenly realised Roy was still talking about the bull.

"A huge Hereford. White-faced. You'd never guess his name in a year of Sundays."

"What was it?"

"They have five children. They take it in turns to name the animals. This time it was little Chrissie's turn to name a new animal. She's three. It must be the only bull in the world glorying in the name of Victoria Semolina."

"They didn't put that on his records," Liam said, not believing a word of it.

Roy smiled.

"Officially, he's Victory Samson. But the children always refer to him as Victoria Semolina. Chrissie apparently is in love with semolina pudding and wishes she'd been called Victoria like her friend down the road. Everyone else calls him Vic, which is OK."

Liam found it as hard to imagine anyone being in love with semolina pudding as it was to imagine it being used as a name. But maybe if you were only three words didn't have quite the same meanings. Perhaps tapioca and spaghetti sounded like the same sort of words as Christine and James. He couldn't even remember being three. You could call kittens names like Tapioca and Spaghetti. He knew a cat called Pizza and a dog called Sherry, and another dog called Teisen which was Welsh for fruit-cake.

Matilda was in the isolation unit in case she brought a germ to the farm that the other animals had never met. She was used to being almost a family pet in her old home, with the children coming to feed and fuss over her every day. Delighted to see people, she ran to the edge of her pen and grunted happily to them.

She was a lovely russet colour, with a much sharper face than most pigs, and flap ears that stood up on her head and pointed forwards, but that moved backwards as she listened when Roy spoke.

Her legs were longer than those of most pigs and so was her sensitive snout. She wrinkled it now at Liam, smelling somebody new. He rubbed her bristly hide and she wriggled in delight.

"It's quite a rare breed now," Roy said.

"Another for my collection. Pity to let the old breeds die."

"They're all so different, really," Liam said. To most people all pigs were alike, but looking at those Roy had bought, some were long and lean and some were small and very fat. Some had long snouts and some had small snouts. Some had relatively long legs and others had stumpy little legs.

"I've another newcomer," Roy said. He opened the second pen in the isolation block. "Noah collected her yesterday. She's due to farrow any time now. Meet Suzanna."

Liam stared at her, unable to believe his eyes. It was the last breed he expected Roy to buy, but if he were collecting unusual breeds, it was just another. It was a breed he adored, a Vietnamese pot-bellied pig.

"They make grand pets so I'm now breeding for the pet market, believe it or not." Roy laughed. "It's amazing what kind of animal suddenly becomes in demand. Easier than dogs. Don't have to take them for walks, though they'd go with you. Clean and good-tempered. House-trained, and like to be with people."

Suzanna lumbered towards him, her

immense tummy almost dragging along the ground.

"She's not quite as big as that normally," Roy said, "but they do have real pot-bellies. For all that they're surprisingly agile." He rubbed her nose. "She's been a pet up to now and lived in the house. Clean as a dog they are. She loves chocolate and sugary biscuits and comes when she's called."

"Why didn't they want her any more?" Liam asked.

"They're having a baby. And so is she. Their baby came along rather unexpectedly, but there's no way they can now cope with a litter of little pigs. They wouldn't have time. Babies take every hour of the day and night and some more you haven't got. So do baby animals. People who've never looked after young things don't know they're born."

"So that's where you are," Josh Murray said, making them both jump as they hadn't heard his approach. "Had to track the voices. I never can find anyone when I come to this place. Got trouble, Noah said."

"One of our little 'uns. Separated her as her mother won't have her and Noah and me's been bottle-feeding her. Think she could have baby pig disease. She's totally apathetic and not feeding at all. Doesn't want to know. I'm very much afraid she's decided life here isn't worth living, after all. But I'd like to save her."

He led the way to Bess's pen.

"Not moved since we saw her," Roy said. The little pig lay there, looking very much as if she would never move again.

"Hmmm." Josh Murray bent over the tiny animal, examining her carefully. "Iron deficiency, I'd say."

"Will that make her better?" Liam asked, watching his father take out a syringe and inject the little animal.

"With any luck. Never can tell when they're so tiny and she really is a titch, isn't she? Pretty little thing. I hope she makes it. Coming home, son?"

"In a tick. I want to see Noah. He promised to lend me a book." It was the only reason he could think of for wanting to see the old man urgently, and he didn't want to tell his father the real reason for seeking out the pigman.

"Can't imagine Noah reading," Josh Murray said. He turned to Roy. "Let's have a look at that pot-bellied pig while we're waiting. She's pretty nearly ready for those babies, isn't she?"

Liam watched them go and then ran to find Noah who was cleaning out the furthest sty.

"How much will that injection be, and the visit?" he asked. "Do you know?"

"Not much change out of fifteen quid, I'd think. Don't know really. Gaffer pays the bills, not me."

"That's my bill," Liam said, wondering how long his money would last if Bess needed many more injections. He joined his father.

"There's a ninety-nine per cent chance that she'll survive," Josh said as they drove out of the farmyard into the lane. That did not stop Liam worrying all the way home.

CHAPTER 7

The worry continued all night. Liam tossed
and turned, trying to think of ways in which he
could make some money and keep his pigs.
Think things through, Grandma said. Look
before you leap. Don't count your chickens
until they're hatched. She and Noah both had
a fund of old sayings which they trotted out
whenever appropriate.

Must be their age, Liam thought. He wasn't
sure how old either of them were, but he
guessed they would have been born about the
same time. Grandma had been part of a world
that was now history. Even pigs were different
when she was a girl, she often said.

He had been counting chickens before they

hatched. He had been thinking of the end result: of pigs for sale, of little pigs, bringing in a small fortune. But it took time for a little pig to grow into a big pig; time for both of them to have all kinds of things wrong with them and his father wouldn't vet them for nothing, even if they were his son's.

"Do you really think the little pig will live?" he asked his father. "I didn't think they were such delicate animals."

"Oddly, they are." Josh Murray was unaware of the reason for his son's worry. "They get heart disease, and problems with their arteries. Maybe because of their size though they aren't fed to be as fat now as they used to be. People want lean bacon and lean meat. They also suffer from stress."

"Stress? What kind of stress?"

"Change worries them, as it does dogs. Animals like routine. It makes them feel safe. Troy's stressed just now, as she's missing Bran and Georgie. She thinks they've gone for ever and can't understand why."

Grandma Bridie was at the Rescue Centre, and the house felt empty without her there.

"Maybe you can start laying the table and preparing our evening meal while I take surgery. Grandma has a lot to do for us and she's not getting any younger. I suspect her arthritis is bad again. She's been very quiet this week."

Suppose Grandma Bridie became ill? How would they manage? Liam had never thought about it before. He supposed that too was part of being older. He had thought that when he grew up worries would go away and he would know how to deal with problems. Instead they just seemed to get bigger and not to have any solution. Grandma wouldn't go on for ever. The whole family relied on her so that Liam's mother Sally could continue her work as a doctor.

He was so busy thinking of his grandmother as unable to do anything for them that he was startled when she bustled into the kitchen.

"I hate people," she announced, putting her coat down on the armchair by the Aga, and pouring boiling water from the kettle that was always on the hob.

"Would you like a coffee, love? I need one before I start on the meal. Thank you for laying the table. That's a big help."

"What's the matter?" Liam asked, guessing that something had happened at the Rescue Centre.

"We get all sorts down there. Dogs, cats, rabbits even. Today two animals came in and I'm ready to spit . . . or worse."

"Why?"

"A young couple brought them in. A cat about two years old. A lovely little animal. She's black and white with green eyes and a delightful disposition. And a little mongrel bitch that's in whelp as they didn't know about seasons. It never occurred to them that this was the time at which she would be mated and then have pups. They let her wander the streets."

Grandma Bridie's small face was indignant.

"The wife's expecting a baby. They say they've had two years' fun out of the animals, and have no further use for them. They can't have them with a baby in the house as they're not hygienic. They want them put to sleep. Only they can't pay a vet and want us to do it."

She took a sip of coffee and almost choked.

"Never mind that they're alive. Never mind that they're healthy. Never mind that they took on the responsibility in the first place. Some people treat animals as if they were toys. Buy them, keep them till they get bored with them, and then get rid of them. People ought to have to sign contracts before they're allowed pets saying 'I promise to care for them to the best of my ability to the end of their natural days.'"

Liam thought of a sticker that was on some of the cars that brought pets to surgery.

A dog is for life, not for Christmas.

He thought of people who had dogs put to sleep before they went on holiday as it was cheaper than paying for kennels, and then bought another puppy when they came home. Next year *it* suffered the same fate. He knew just how his grandmother felt.

He hadn't believed his father when he told him, but he knew now that it was true.

Grandma Bridie finished her coffee. Liam didn't know what to say. He shared her anger. People had no right to take on pets if they didn't intend to keep them for always.

"Will you find homes for them?"

"I've brought the cat back for Lois. She's been complaining about mice and rats in the feed store. The little bitch will stay till she's reared her pups and then we'll have to find homes for all of them." She slammed a plate of pasties down on to the table. "There's more nonsense talked about animals being unhygienic than there is about almost anything else. Children need animals; need to learn how to care for them and how to be gentle and sensible. Otherwise they grow up knowing very little about real life."

Real life was out on the farm, Liam thought, wishing he could bring Porgy and Bess home and look after them by himself. Five weeks before school began.

He could spend most days with Roy.

"School soon," Grandma Bridie said, as if five weeks ended tomorrow. "Have you started your project? It will take lots of time to do it properly."

His project!

He had forgotten all about it. They had to write about any special events that had occurred during the holiday. He had nothing to write about except the pigs.

A project on pigs.

Why not? He could say he spent all his time on Roy's farm, which was almost true. He spent all the time that mattered to him there. As soon as the meal was over he raced upstairs to find the notebook he had bought. He'd have to think hard and spend all the evening working, and maybe several more evenings.

What did he know about pigs?

Noah said they came from wild pigs, long

ago. They had several sources. The pigs found in Europe were long and rangy with narrow heads, and were the colour of a shabby fox. Others came from China and parts of Asia and were small with short legs and had soft-haired hides.

The imported pigs weren't very strong, and people began to cross them with other breeds. Noah had always been fascinated by the old breeds, breeds he said that everyone had forgotten.

What had Roy said about pig breeding? Liam racked his brains, wishing he had made notes. He'd have to go over and talk to Noah and Roy and that would be difficult as they were always rushing somewhere to do something important.

He had books on breeding and rearing, nothing on their history. That would be important to Roy if he started keeping rare breeds. He'd have people who expected to be told all about each one. Pigs could be for bacon, dual purpose, or for pork. It all depended on the type and the way they were reared.

They could be pedigree or hybrid. Noah always swore that a first-generation cross in any animal made for immense improvements, but to go on after that brought problems. Hybrid vigour, he called it. Which wasn't the same as mongrels.

Those were a mishmash of many different breeds. A hybrid was from two different pedigree animals.

The Guide Dog people crossed yellow Labradors and golden Retrievers to get strong healthy dogs, without some of the faults you might get in either breed. Liam thought about the word yellow as he wrote it. So many people called them golden Labradors and they weren't. Get it right, his father said. Yellow is right.

He suddenly wondered why you only saw black pups or yellow pups, never a mixture, though both could crop up in the same litter.

He wrote that many people used an incorrect description, in case his teacher thought he was using the wrong name. No Labrador breeder would ever get it wrong, nor would anyone who knew about dogs and their breeds.

The Guide Dog people didn't go on breeding from the pups. So it would be the same with pigs.

Breeding was much more complicated than people thought. It was also exciting. Major Simms had a stud dog called Ruff. Liam had seen some of his puppies. They were all so different, yet every one inherited their father's wonderful calm character. The mothers were always very carefully chosen. Nothing haphazard.

Liam picked up one of the books on breeding.

Selection of good, sound, healthy stock was essential. Close breeding might produce faults of all kinds. Liam suddenly remembered a story his father had told about one of his clients. That could go into his project too.

There had been an epidemic of swine fever and all the farms in the district were quarantined, which meant that nobody could mate their sows with boars from another farm. One farm had mated their prize boar to one of his daughters. Every single piglet had been deformed and they had all had to be put to sleep.

"Problems on both sides and it came out," Josh Murray said, when telling the story. "Inbreeding makes for some very odd results. I don't like it. It can make for very hysterical puppies."

"Happens in people too," Maldwyn, his father's partner had added. Liam remembered a bitch in the hospital that had been mated to her own father. All her pups had died soon after birth. "The old pharaohs always married brother to sister and some strange things came out then in the children."

Pigs could fight, sometimes in the litters, but nearly always if two separate litters were mixed. If they had to mix them they were given sedatives, Suicalm. Very safe, his father said, always carrying some in his bag, so that if he had a pig patient he could quieten it before treating it.

Liam looked through his postcard collection. He had pictures of almost every breed of pig in existence. Large White. Welsh which were a little smaller than the Middle White, who were very good mothers. That breed was almost extinct, but Noah said that just a few specimens could be found on some farms. Large Black, British Saddleback, Berkshire, Gloucester Old Spot, Tamworth, British Landrace.

They came from different parts of the country, looked different. Some had flop ears that almost hid their eyes and some had erect ears. The Gloucester Old Spot belonged in the South of England and was one of the best for outdoor feeding, as it enjoyed eating grass.

He began to think of Porgy and Bess. Young female pigs were called gilts, so Bess was a gilt, till she'd had her first litter. Roy didn't like animals being bred too young, so she'd be about a year old when she went to the boar, and her babies would be born about sixteen weeks later.

She could have two litters a year for five years at least. If she had ten piglets each time, and she could have more, that would be twenty piglets a year. Over a hundred in her breeding life. He wondered what the selling price of pigs was. Even if it was only ten pounds apiece, and it had to be more than that, that was a thousand pounds.

If he kept some of her daughters . . .

Only there was food and housing and vet bills to pay. He looked out at the big paddock, just beyond the garden of the House of Secrets, visualising it covered with small sties with curved roofs, and pigs and piglets running free among them.

They could surely divide it, so that Lois had room for her horses in one half and he had the other half. He'd only need half an acre. If they were down at the far end where there were oak trees there'd also be acorns for them. Free food.

There were only three horses, and Freya's foal. Georgie had taken Lindsay and her foal with her. Rocket, Fortune and Freya and her baby, Nymph, were mostly in the stables in the winter.

If only Bess survived . . .

No use daydreaming. He'd better get on with his project or he'd be in trouble. What could he call it? The Successful Pig Farm?

He began to look at the equipment needed. There'd be more problems than he'd realised. Little pigs escaped. An electric fence would prevent that, but it would also cost money.

He turned to another book.

The number of piglets in a litter could vary from one or two to twenty. Only the sow couldn't feed more than ten well so you needed several sows to have their babies at the same time. Then you could give those with a few babies some of those from sows that had too many. If you could make her accept those that weren't hers.

They needed to be mixed in while she was having them, and she needed to be sedated. It was all very complicated.

Two piglets in a litter wouldn't pay for much; twenty would cause enormous problems if you only had one sow. Especially if you were only thirteen and still at school. There was no way he could manage if he brought them home. He needed Roy and Noah, and the sows that Roy had, as some of them could take extra babies.

He was counting chickens again.

He turned to a veterinary handbook on keeping pigs that he had borrowed from the surgery. He wished he hadn't. The list of diseases was endless. It was even worse for baby pigs, listed under piglet mortality. Porgy and Bess would never survive.

Bess had piglet anaemia. She could survive with treatment. She would be better if turned outside on grass.

"What on earth are you up to?" Liam's father asked from the doorway. "Do you know the time?"

Liam had forgotten about the clock. It was after ten and he ought to have been in bed.

"I'm doing my holiday project. I'd forgotten all about it. I'm writing about Roy's pig farm. I can't think of anything else to do. Dad, what did you inject into the little piglet?"

"Only vitamin E. Roy's giving her feeds containing iron and cobalt; my own mixture. She has a quarter of a teaspoonful every day for the next few days. Time you were in bed, son."

Liam went to bed, but lay awake for a long time, his mind full of facts about pigs. He hoped his teacher would enjoy reading them. Nobody else was likely to choose such an unusual subject.

The moon swung up the sky. There the stars looked down on him. Sleep seemed a million miles away too. He sighed and lifted the lid of his musical box. The little tinkling notes sang softly through the room. He wondered if Orpheus had enchanted pigs as well as other animals.

Half asleep, he realised there were other things he could put into the project. It could have a broader basis than just Roy's farm. The pig in fact and fiction; the pig today and yesterday.

There were the Gadarene swine in the Bible. He'd have to look them up as he didn't remember anything about them except the name. In the *Iliad* the witch Circe had turned all of Odysseus's men into swine.

In the Middle Ages men were hung for stealing pigs. An old rhyme suddenly came into his head:

Tom, Tom, the piper's son
Stole a pig and away did run.
Tom was beat and the pig was eat
And Tom went howling down the street.

Liam wondered who had beaten him. If it was his father, it wasn't very fair to eat the pig he'd stolen and beat him for it.

He wished he could fall asleep. His brain was whirling.

Pigs . . . a lot of religions regarded them as unclean animals. Jews and Muslims didn't eat them. Liam wondered why. He suddenly remembered his father commenting on that after he had read a book about Ancient Egypt.

The Nile delta had been very rich land, and the natives kept sheep, goats and pigs. They enjoyed pork although it was forbidden by the priests as food. They thought pork belonged to Set, who was one of the wickedest gods.

You thought of history as battles and laws, but it wasn't. It was people and the way they lived. Would the Egyptians be punished for eating pork if the priests caught them? What sort of punishments would there be in Ancient Egypt?

I want to get to sleep, Liam thought crossly, but still he lay awake.

Major Simms had been there the night Georgie showed them that she could walk and ride. They had talked about ancient customs, after his father had told them about the book he was reading.

They had had roast pork for supper. That was how the conversation began. His father had been out to the abattoir and had brought home some meat for the freezer.

"Just as well the Celts didn't have that sort of god," Major Simms said. "They had enormous feasts of roast pork. Their warriors, after a successful battle, were given a whole thigh of a wild boar or an entire roast piglet. They called it the hero's portion. They washed it down with great quantities of ale, and had to sleep for twenty-four hours to recover."

He laughed.

"That was probably the time that enemies attacked. Men drunk with ale and stupid with eating wouldn't offer much resistance. They had great feasts in those days. We seem to have lost the custom."

"Perhaps it's as well," Grandma Bridie said. "I could never eat vast quantities knowing half the world is starving."

Liam wondered what sort of quantity Grandma considered vast as she was famous for her ample helpings.

Thinking about Bess, Liam found himself unable to contemplate eating a roast piglet. They had looked after a turkey once in the surgery. It had pneumonia. He had been a small boy then. The farmer had offered it to them for Christmas after as they had cured it. He'd known that turkey well. They had to buy one from the shop, as he had refused to eat Christmas dinner if they ate Susie.

Roy always said that when he ate his own pigs he knew they had been well cared for, treated well and died so quickly that they knew nothing about it. They had to die in the end and old age often brought suffering. They were spared that.

It didn't seem to worry Roy or Noah at all. Liam fell asleep at last, and for the next few days he irritated Grandma Bridie immensely by becoming vegetarian. It made life impossible, she declared, having to prepare different meals for him, and also to find out what to cook, so that his health didn't suffer.

"You get used to it, son," Noah said, as Liam looked at Bess, now recovered and lively as before. "Everything in nature has some use. I reckon there's a pattern and we ignore it at our peril. Leads to all sorts of things, as when an animal becomes extinct the pattern changes. We don't know what place they have in the world."

He paused to load a spadeful of muck into the wheelbarrow, as he was cleaning out Colossus's sty.

"Kill off the insect-eating birds, and we have a plague of horrible stinging things we never had before. Kill off all the cats and we're overrun with mice and rats and plague will come back. Kill off the foxes and there's plagues of rabbits eating all the food we grow, so we go hungry."

He lifted the handles of the barrow.

"Everything has a purpose. If we interfere, we upset the balance. Remember that, young Liam." He trundled off, and Liam sat and tickled Bess's ears and she grunted happily to him. She had made a complete recovery after Josh's treatment. Porgy, jealous, butted her away and rubbed himself against the side of the pen, asking for attention in his turn.

CHAPTER 8

The days passed fast. The holiday seemed to be speeding towards its end. The piglets grew. Liam had never realised before how fast they grew. They were mischievous and they were active and Porgy was the liveliest small animal about the farm, with an unquenchable curiosity, so that if he could escape he did.

Liam needed to know far more about pigs. He borrowed his father's veterinary dictionary and then wished he hadn't.

Pigs could get flu, especially the little pigs. He had visions of all his money vanishing in vet bills. You could insure dogs against vet bills; could you insure pigs?

He asked Noah, who laughed.

"Maybe insure a good boar against death, but never heard of anyone insuring every pig he had against vet bills. Cost more than the bills, I'd reckon," the old man said.

Liam sighed.

"I'm doing a project on pigs," he said.

"Tell you a couple of stories," Noah said, sitting companionably beside Liam as he watched Bess and Porgy guzzling. Porgy always liked to put his feet in his trough. Bess pushed him away crossly as she was sure her food was better than his.

"There was a pig once who saved a little girl from drowning. Swam into the water and the child hung on to her. The sow got a medal."

"You're joking."

"Honest, I'm not. True as I sit here. Read it in a book of unusual rescues, but can't remember the title. There was another pig they used to detect drugs. Good as dogs, they are, but they get a bit big. Couldn't get one of our prize sows into a small sitting room or on a boat without a lot of difficulty."

Liam chuckled at the thought of Delilah or Dainty, who was one of the biggest pigs he'd ever seen, hunting round a small boat to see if it carried an illegal cargo. It would go into his project though. He hoped it was true and that Noah wasn't pulling his leg.

Just to make sure, he asked Roy.

"I've read about both of them," he assured Liam. "Pigs are much cleverer than people realise. After all, if they can smell truffles, they are just as likely to smell drugs. Their noses are as good as a dog's, any day."

He spent more time now at the farm than at home.

"Come and see Mrs P," Roy said.

Mrs P was short for Mrs Pankhurst, who had been one of the most awkward and persistent of the early suffragettes. Mrs P the pig was also noisy, awkward and persistent. Nobody could ever ignore her.

She was always demanding her rights. When other pigs were fed, Mrs Pankhurst screamed to be first. If she were taken out of her pen and led elsewhere, she went anywhere but in the right direction. If people persisted in annoying her, she butted them.

When she was taken to the boar she wouldn't go in the van and when she came home she wouldn't get out of it. She sat in her feed if she could manage it, and if not put her feet in it. She upset her water pail until Roy installed a push button for her to press for a drink. She then flooded her sty.

"Thought so," said Roy with considerable satisfaction, as they walked into the sty. "I only hope she manages sensibly and doesn't think of something outrageous to do with her babies."

The sow had begun to produce her first litter. That could always be difficult as she had no idea what was happening to her and some sows were so overwhelmed that they attacked their babies, never having seen tiny pigs before.

Liam had never realised birth could be so easy or so fast. The first little pig was almost there. Within seconds he was out, and on his feet. He was no bigger than one of his mother's ears. He stood at once, and, unlike lambs or foals, was able to run within seconds of being born.

He trotted round to the front of his mother. She looked at him and grunted and he looked at her, his expression amazed.

Roy laughed.

"It never fails to amuse me," he said. "It's the first thing they all do. Run round and have a look at Mum and look utterly astounded. Imagine being born into the sty, and seeing the world they inherit. I wonder what they make of it all. I often wonder what pigs think we are, other than being their providers and carers."

"Heigh-ho, big girl," Noah said, doing one of his genie-like appearances, and neatly fielding another little pig that Mrs P appeared to be trying to squash against the side of the pen. The piglet followed her brother, who had now found a teat and fastened himself to it. She too stared up at the sow, who put her nose forward and pushed at the tiny animal.

"Number three," said Noah, as another little female piglet trotted through the straw. "I wonder what they make of us too. Always remember working on a farm long ago when three pigs got into the garden. Found them with their noses pressed against the window of the dining room, staring in. You never saw any animal look so amazed."

"Chairs and tables. Wallpaper and pictures. So that's how people live! Wonder if they see what we do." Roy laughed again. "Remember that afternoon when Silver led the herd into the estate?"

"Aye," Noah said. "That was before the days of milk quotas. You could sell as much milk as you could produce. Now there are new regulations. Each dairy farm has a limit on the amount of milk they may sell. It has halved farm incomes for many dairy farmers. Life was easy then." He sighed. Roy only kept one Jersey cow for milk for them. He had sold his herd to concentrate on pigs when quotas first began.

"What happened?" Liam asked. Both Roy and Noah had an annoying habit of starting a story and then rushing off to feed pigs or clean out a sty.

"Might as well tell you, though it's a long story. I don't want to leave Mrs P on her own. Nasty habit of lying on piglets, sows have. Clumsy things."

"I'll bring sandwiches and coffee," Noah said, vanishing through the door.

"Silver?" Liam prompted.

"Silver was a a large and awkward Friesian cow. She was the herd boss and had to go into the milking parlour first. If she didn't and another cow went in, she just went in and tried to push her out. I once had a student vet here who was doing farming work in his vacation, and he got caught between the two of them."

Roy chuckled.

"Silver and Goldie and young Sam all ended up in one compartment. Took us an hour to get them out and poor Sam was in a mess when at last we managed it. Silver just wouldn't budge. She was a stickler for routine. Milking at four was a hard and fast rule. The trouble was that we put the clocks backwards and forwards in March and October and it messes everything up. Usually I just changed milking time, but that day I'd forgotten the clocks had changed. Four o'clock was at what had been five o'clock the day before."

He paused to extricate another tiny piglet from beneath his mother.

"It doesn't seem to bother her at all," Liam said, as a sixth popped out and started her trek to the front of the sow.

"They're so small compared with her that probably she feels very little. Sows rarely make a fuss, or have problems, other than lying on the litter," Roy said. "Where was I?"

"Late for milking," Liam said.

"Silver decided we'd forgotten, but she hadn't. She managed to lift the latch on the gate and she led the herd through. Down the road and up an alleyway and, for some reason known only to her, she diverted into a small suburban garden."

Roy lifted a squealing piglet that had lost

himself in the straw and tucked him against his mother.

"I'd gone down to the field and found it empty and was looking for them so didn't get the message to come at first." He grinned. "By the time I got there, there was this garden about eighty metres long, with all my herd in it. You never saw such a mess. One cow appeared to be trying to climb an apple tree. Half the neighbours had come in to try and get them out into the road again and the police had been called."

He stopped to count the piglets. There were now nine. Noah came back with huge hunks of bread and lumps of cheese, a jar of pickles and a flask of coffee and three mugs. He put them down on a bench at the side of the sty. Liam was starving. The cheese was wonderful with a rare bite to it, and the bread was home-made and new.

"Alice's bread and Darrow Farm cheese from their barn shop," Noah said, biting into it with satisfaction. "Not like factory-made stuff, without any taste at all."

"How did you get the cows out?" Liam asked, thinking about a small garden with a large herd filling it, as well as people and policemen.

"With extreme difficulty. It might have been easy if it hadn't turned into a circus. One policeman had turned up and panicked and asked for reinforcements. He'd seen Wild West films and was chasing a cow through a flower-bed with a bit of clothes line, trying to lasso her. She panicked and knocked down the fence and fled through the gardens, with him in hot pursuit. Not sure what he'd have done if he'd caught her."

He paused to bite heartily into bread and cheese and pickles, and to finish chewing. Mrs P grunted massively and produced her tenth piglet.

"For some reason the extra police had come in a Black Maria. There were about five of them. One of the neighbours had made coffee and everyone stopped for a drink and Silver and I glared at one another. Then I remembered she loved chocolate so someone found me a Milky Bar."

It began to rain outside, drumming on the sty roof. Lightning flashed. Thunder rumbled in the distance.

"The last thing we need," Roy said crossly. "Mess up the hay. I ought to have got it in, but I haven't."

Liam took another doorstep of bread, cut himself a piece of cheese and added pickles.

"Silver took one sniff at the chocolate and followed me, out of the garden, down the side path, through the front garden and into the street. Because she was boss cow the others followed her, except for the panic-driven straggler that was now six gardens away, having demolished a tiny apple tree and a lilac as well as the fences. I got the herd back into the yard and Noah started milking while I went to find Pansy."

He took more bread and cheese.

"Luckily she knew me well and was scared of the stupid policeman, who she probably thought was going to attack her when he caught up with her and she followed me home. Made a mess of those gardens, though."

"Had a funny sequel," Noah said.

Liam couldn't wait. The story sounded more and more improbable and there couldn't be any more.

"What was it?" he asked.

"I went shopping a few days later and met a lady who lived in one of the houses. She'd had an operation and come home that day and was resting in her chair. I asked if she felt better."

Liam was puzzled as that seemed to have little to do with cows.

Noah saw his expression and winked at Roy, his little wizened face looking gnomelike.

"Think he'll believe it?" he asked.

"What did happen? What did she say?" Liam knew there was more to the story than that.

"She said that she'd been having an after-dinner rest, and then discovered that the medicine she was taking produced visions. She thought she saw a cow's head race past her window, followed by a policeman's head in his helmet."

"Well, she had," said Liam.

"Ah, yes, but it wasn't very likely, was it? Not in a suburban garden with no cows near, so far as she knew. It didn't occur to her to look out of the window. If she had, she'd have seen the mess they made. So she said she took a large glass of brandy and went to bed. She was very worried all afternoon in case she had more visions, but nothing happened. She wasn't well enough to go out into the garden. Her husband discovered the fence at the end was pushed down and there were signs of cow all over the top end of the lawn."

Liam laughed this time.

"It must have been an awful shock for the poor woman," he said. "And a terrific relief when she discovered she hadn't been seeing things!"

"I'm not sure which upset her most," Roy said. "The cow or the policeman."

He glanced at his watch. The thunder rumbles were dying away in the distance and the rain had eased.

"Work to do," he said. "Can you stay with Mrs P, Noah? I suspect there might be one or two more to come."

Liam counted. There were now twelve little pigs, most of them feeding, but three were sound asleep near their mother's head. They were so small and so pink. Incredible little things, full of life as soon as they were born, not blind like puppies and kittens, having to learn to walk and run.

"Time for my new baby," Roy said, leading the way to the cottage where the Arab mare lived with her foal. "Had to tell Noah. He wanted to see the shires' new quarters. He didn't approve at first. Said we're pig farmers, not horse breeders."

"Did he change his mind?" Liam asked.

"Quickly, when he heard what I'm getting

for the foal when I sell him. Best spot of diversification I ever did, he said."

"What does diversify really mean?" Liam asked.

"Doing something different. Farming doesn't pay any more. Prices vary, too many rules and regulations that stop you from growing what you want and selling it all. So farmers are doing all sorts of things. Having farm shops. Breeding exotic animals. Letting cottages for holiday-makers or turning barns into holiday homes. Opening to the public, which I'm going to do. Charge them to visit the museum, and to see the rare breeds. I think the mare would interest people, don't you?"

Liam had an idea, but he intended to keep that secret even from Roy. There was a way he could maybe repay the farmer for keeping his two pigs for him. Both now knew him when he came to visit and ran to him when he had the bottle. Bess was remarkably active, jumping over Porgy if he were lying down. Occasionally she scrambled over him and he stood up, indignant, and she fell off and squealed and butted him crossly.

Kazra walked delicately towards them when Roy opened the stable door. She stretched out her head for the apple he held in his hand. Haroun, no longer timid, came and butted Roy's shoulder, complaining because he hadn't had his apple first.

"He's worth several thousand pounds," Roy said. "My treasure trove. Everything I have is tied up in those two."

"You said you'd sold him. Why hasn't he gone to his new owner?"

"He's moving over to Ireland next spring. He's already paid for the youngster, and believe me, Haroun is heavily insured. I'm being paid to look after him until the new premises are ready."

Roy filled the haynets, checking to ensure that they were safely hung and could not fall and tangle with the horses' legs.

"Haroun is paying for our extensions, the new stables, doing up this cottage, and the farm museum, as well as all the notices that will guide people to us when we open to the public."

Farming was a very expensive occupation, Liam thought, as Roy shut the stable doors and padlocked them. There was a new burglar alarm on the wall, and security lights as well.

"Can't be too careful," Roy said. "I can see

the lights flash on from my bedroom window. They wake me up. Though so far they've been triggered by one of the cats or a fox. I'll be happier when the new stable is built beside the house. Not so far to come in case of trouble."

"Do you expect trouble?"

"Just as well to be careful these days," Roy said. "I'll be glad when I get the two dogs. They're due early October."

Back at the farm Mrs P had decided twelve piglets was enough for any one mother. She was stretched out on her side with everyone, according to Noah, plugged in.

"Eight female, four male," Noah said. "How's that project of yours coming along?"

"It's growing fast," Liam said, looking down at the vast sow. "Will Bess be as big as that?"

"If you're lucky. Roy's off tomorrow on the track of more of his rare breeds. Some of them died right out, more's the pity."

"Like what?" Liam asked.

"The Small White. Tiny and as fat as butter. So fat it couldn't move, so maybe just as well it's gone. People liked very fat pigs right up to the 1960s when they discovered that too much fat in the diet is bad for people. They crossed the Small White with the Large White and got the Middle White. There are a few of those still around. Another very fat little pig, so fat it was more like a ball than an animal, judging by the old pictures, was the Dorset Gold Tip."

"Funny name," Liam said. "It sounds more like a butterfly." Several piglets detached themselves and were huddled together away from their mother, under the infra-red lamp.

"Funny animals," Noah said. "No loss to anyone. They had to put lumps of wood under their snouts to stop them suffocating themselves when they were asleep."

Liam wondered whether he could include that in his project. He had a feeling his teacher might not believe him. He was not sure that he believed it.

He must have nearly enough material now to write it all up. He went out into the farmyard, where Greg was stalking a long piece of straw that was blowing in the wind. Beyond him two of his kittens teased one another, chasing over the hay bales, now one and then the other standing on top, batting down at her sister.

It was time to go home.

CHAPTER 9

Liam always found school work difficult, as much of it failed to capture his interest. The project had seemed tedious at first, a distracting nuisance, but as he began to write down all he knew about pigs he became more and more fascinated. He could understand farming and living with animals. The library, which he rarely used, proved a rich source of material, and he began to explore the shelves.

He was up early, to walk Troy. He went over to the farm to look at his pigs. His father or grandmother drove him, so that Troy could come too. She was as interested as Liam in watching Porgy and Bess learning to drink milk from their little troughs, and scramble around the pen together.

Porgy was a busy, inquisitive little animal, and he enjoyed jumping.

"Make a show-jumper, that one," Noah said, as he raised the side of the pen yet again because Porgy had jumped over it. Bess, unable to follow him, put her small front trotters on the wall and squealed her annoyance.

Liam had never worked so hard in all his life, but he didn't realise he was working. It was such fun. Time flew past. Noah helped him with his project and so did Roy, dredging information out of their minds, guiding him back through the past, telling him where to search for more knowledge.

He had never done well at school. His reports were average, never as good as any of the others. He accepted that Jenna and the twins were much cleverer than he. Now he was inspired, feeling a seething ambition to produce the best project anyone had ever done, to find out more than anyone else about his favourite animals and their history, and show everyone he wasn't so dumb after all.

He was on a quest and the quest in itself was exciting.

In Norman times the nobles hunted the wild boar. The animals were nothing like today's pigs. They were long and lean and mean-looking, with bristles and small angry eyes in sharp-nosed heads. Not a beast to tangle with unless you were well armed.

They helped to keep the forests from becoming choked with undergrowth that killed the trees. Noah gave him a cutting from the newspaper. It was an item about pigs that were put into woodland to graze it, and described how they cleared bracken and other unwanted vegetation, letting in light and air and allowing tree seedlings to grow.

"If there were no farms, the country would be nothing but scrubland and marsh," Noah said. "Humans make the landscape what it is. They tame the jungle and tidy it. They feed the land and shape it. In Britain the woodlands and forests are mostly managed. The wild places breed danger. We don't want acres of bramble and bracken and nothing else."

Liam thought of a field near his home. The owner had died and nobody farmed it now. It was shoulder-high with thistle and sorrel, with bracken and ragwort, an eyesore amongst the other fields that belonged to the farms around and were trim and tilled, or grazed by cattle and sheep and horses.

The animals had their place in keeping chaos at bay. They always had. But man hunted them to extinction and then left a gap, as no other animal ate the same food or behaved in the same way. Wild boar had kept the countryside from being choked with jungle, and too much hunting had been prevented so that they continued to breed.

The people who lived then knew how important it was to keep the woods clear and free of choking undergrowth that prevented the trees from growing.

The wild boar were protected by game laws, and only the very rich were allowed to eat them. They fed in the forests. Nobody put out food for them. Liam wondered if they scavenged round human houses.

No food for animals in the winter; and maybe not a lot for humans, as there were no freezers. Salt meat and dried vegetables for stews. Bread. He suddenly remembered his father and a friend one evening talking about the Irish potato famine when people starved to death and began to emigrate to America because they had no food. They lived on potatoes and milk.

But if you couldn't feed the cows in winter, they were killed and salted, and then you didn't have milk.

Among other meats, there would be wild boars. The wild sows made nests of grass or bracken. Roy's pigs liked to try and make nests of straw.

"That's how you know the litter's nearly due," Roy said.

Animals might change in shape but instincts didn't change.

He needed more books. He was so engrossed that Grandma had to come and find him for meals, as they had suddenly become unimportant.

"Hope you're not sickening for something," she said, suspicious of this sudden lack of appetite, though Liam ate well enough once he remembered the food was on the table.

"Just doing my project," he said, and cycled off to the library again. There were only two books on pigs, one a long tome for farmers and one a small and funny book by someone who had taken up pig farming for the first time.

Noah found an old book at home called the Backyard Pig Farmer that his daughter had picked up in a jumble sale.

The day before school began again Liam was busy writing when his father put his head round the door.

"Trouble," he said. "Can you come and help?"

"What's wrong?"

"Remember I told you I was visiting the Downhurst Kennels today? Tanya, one of the German Shepherds, is about to whelp."

Liam nodded.

"She's due to have pups in the next two days. She got out of the kennels. Someone left the gate open and she's vanished. Apart from anything else those pups are valuable and Tanya isn't the best of mothers. Have you watched Bran track with Troy?"

Liam looked at his father, puzzled by what seemed to be a change of subject.

"Yes, often. He showed me how to make a track before he went away. I've not done it with her. I think I know how."

"We can hardly ask the police to spare a dog to track Tanya. Miss Fenton wondered if Troy might do it."

That was even more exciting than his project. Liam put his books away and called Troy, taking her tracking harness and line off the

128

brass pig which had eight hooks on it and held all the things he needed for her.

She adored tracking. It was her favourite occupation and she had missed it since Bran went away. She danced round Liam, wildly excited, barking in a shrill high voice that she never used at any other time. "I'm going to track, I'm going to track, I'm going to track," her body shouted as soon as Liam took hold of the harness.

She was outside in a moment, prancing by the Land Rover, impatient for the door to be opened. The second it was opened, she was in, sitting on the floor at the rear of the vehicle, mouth open, tongue hanging out, her eyes laughing.

Liam felt guilty. If he had done a few tracks with her, she might not have fretted so much for Bran.

"Why would Tanya run away?" he asked his father, as they negotiated the narrow lanes, where honeysuckle grew thick in the hedges that nobody ever cut these days.

"Bitches often want to be alone with their pups, not in a place that's busy. She'll have gone to look for somewhere quiet, maybe dug herself a hole, to have them there. It's an instinct left over from the wild dog."

Like Roy's pigs making straw nests, Liam thought.

Liam had not visited the Downhurst Kennels before. The one-time farmhouse stood stark against the landscape, unsheltered by trees. It was a bleak-looking building. Dogs in runs barked at them. Tanya's owner was waiting for them, her expression anxious.

"Tanya has trouble with her pups at the best of times," she said. "One of the kennel girls forgot to latch her kennel door properly. Tanya saw her chance. She did this once before, but we managed to catch her before she got to the gate. This time everything was against us, as the van delivering our month's supply of dog food had turned up. He left the gate open. We were unloading the food into the barn. No one saw her go."

Liam was putting on Troy's harness. It was made of leather, with stiff straps that went round her chest and under her legs. It was like a jigsaw puzzle and she wasn't helping by her impatience.

At last the buckles were done up, and the long line that attached her to him was clipped in place.

"Which way did Tanya go before?" asked Josh Murray.

"Towards the river. That way." Alison Fenton, who owned the kennels, pointed to a narrow track that led among gorse bushes across a common.

Liam took Troy back to Tanya's kennel, and let her sniff around for a few minutes.

"Find Tanya," he said, taking her to the little path. She put her nose down, and sniffed along the trail for a yard or so, and then looked back at him, baffled.

Liam wished he had paid more attention when he was watching Bran work her. He had never realised that tracking could be useful, that Troy might do it for a real reason, not just a game. People got lost. Children got lost. Tanya was lost, and Troy had a skill he didn't know how to use.

She was looking for scent on the ground. He remembered that. Scent of broken grass and crushed plants where the bitch had walked. Scent of Tanya's paws, scent from hairs that she might have shed. Scent of tiny insects she had trodden on. All of it made sense to the dog, Bran said. Why hadn't he listened harder?

Why hadn't he realised just what a wonderful talent Troy had?

Dogs' noses are so much more sensitive than human noses, identifying the tiniest traces. The smell of drugs, hidden deep in a cargo. The smell of an unseen bomb. The scent of a lost climber, hurt on the hills. Dogs were used to detect gas leaks and oil leaks, deep underground, Bran had told him. They could smell gas when meters failed to detect the leak. He had stored the information away as interesting but not of much use.

"She doesn't know what we want," he said.

"I don't think it's that. Try the other side of the road, Liam," Alison Fenton said. "She can't track Tanya if she didn't go that way."

The path on the other side of the road led through even thicker gorse. Quite suddenly Troy put her nose down, and began to pull so hard that Liam could scarcely keep up with her. He felt a sudden wild thrill, an excitement that he had never experienced before. Troy was reading the ground, was taking news from it of things that he could only guess at.

He hoped that she really was tracking Tanya, and not after fox or badger or rabbit. A turn to the side and a quick sniff. Liam looked at the grass. Feathers lay there, telling of a kill the day before. Fox or hawk had pounced and some small bird had suffered.

She dived off to the side of the track again, smelling intently. The grass was flattened. Perhaps Tanya had stopped to rest.

Liam had never known anything quite like this before. It was deeply satisfying, bonding him to Troy in a way he had never experienced. She was his dog, and he wanted, passionately, to find Tanya, so that he could write and tell Bran about it.

It would be a triumph, but there was more to it than that.

Working with the dog, he hoped desperately that they would find Tanya before she had her pups and could take her home to safety. The pups were at risk from fox and stoat and weasel, and Tanya would have to fight for their safety.

She would also have to hunt and feed herself and she had never done that in her life. She was used to warmth and shelter and people to care for her.

Troy turned off at an angle. She was now almost running, and Liam tripped over a bramble root and fell. He dropped the line and the dog was away, speeding over the ground. The thin rope, which was fifteen metres long, trailed behind her and caught on a tree, so that she pulled up short, yelping in frustration.

Alison Fenton shot forward as, from apparently nowhere, a large black German Shepherd launched herself in fury at Troy. Within moments the two bitches were scrapping frenziedly. Liam's father raced from behind, taking off his anorak as he ran. He dropped it over the contestants, and there was a sudden silence. Alison pulled Tanya by her collar, and separated her, still snarling, from Troy, who shook her head, spattering blood from a torn ear.

From the ground near by came the sound of frantic small whimpers.

Liam fastened the lead that was in his pocket on to Troy's collar. She sat, panting. The bite on her ear would need stitching but she seemed otherwise unharmed.

Josh Murray walked forward and put his arm into the hole in the ground.

"Five pups, all alive," he said, bringing them out one by one. Tanya was struggling to get to them.

"She has more to come," Alison said. "She isn't fit to walk back. That fight hasn't done her any good either. She's not hurt, but she's very upset."

"She thought Troy might harm her pups," Josh said. "I'll carry her back. Luckily it isn't too far. You and Liam carry the pups. Tuck them into your anoraks. Liam ought to be able to manage two, if Troy will behave herself."

Troy had to behave herself, Liam thought. It was suddenly important. In those few minutes while he was behind her, watching her work, something had happened to make him feel differently towards the dog. Before she had been Bran's and he was just looking after her. Suddenly she was his and he was passionate about her.

She nosed his hand, worried, lest he were angry with her. The fight had not been her fault, as she had only defended herself against a hurtling demon that sprang out of the ground. She was in pain from her ear, and puzzled, as she had never been attacked before. Nor had she smelled puppies before. She knew that something was different, and did not know if she were to blame. She walked quietly, afraid she had done wrong, careful not to pull or lag.

Back at the kennels Alison took Tanya into

her own bed, and settled her with the pups. Josh examined mother and babies. As he did so yet another pup was born, lying on the bedding, covered in a gleaming membrane. Tanya lifted her baby gently with her teeth and laid it upside down on her crossed paws, before licking the head free, and then licking the rest of the small squirming body.

"She's learned in the past few years," Alison Fenton said thankfully. "She was awkward with her first two litters, but she seems to be enjoying this one."

The other pups were feeding.

"She's got away with it," Josh said, after a careful examination. "She could have been very unlucky. Like last time."

"What happened last time?" Liam asked. "I thought you caught her in time."

"We did, but the first pup had been born and we didn't know it. By the time we found him, six hours later, down by the side of the barn, he was dead. It was very cold that day, and he hadn't been cleaned up or fed. I don't think he ever managed to breathe. It was a shame. He was a lovely puppy." Alison Fenton sighed. "You win some. You lose some."

A few minutes later she said, "I'm sorry

about Troy. She didn't deserve that after finding Tanya for us. It was very clever of her."
One of the kennel girls had brought a pad of tissues that Liam was holding against his dog's ear. She looked forlorn, and needed a wash to get the blood off her coat.

"Not a lot we can do with it at the moment," Josh said. "It will have to be stitched. We'll get her home. I don't think Tanya needs me at the moment, but ring if there's a problem."

"Seven pups now and all's well at the moment," Alison said, from the kennel door, as they walked over to the Land Rover. "Sorry about your little bitch, Liam. I hope it won't upset her with other dogs."

"Could it?" Liam asked his father, holding the pad of tissues to Troy's ear as they drove home.

"It might have done when she was younger," his father said. "I think she's old enough now to realise that most dogs don't go for her as soon as they see her. She may even understand about the pups and that Tanya was just protecting them. After all, she didn't know we were with Troy, who might have been a stray and harmed the babies."

That night, when Troy's ear had been

stitched, she followed Liam up to his room and lay down at his feet. He bent to stroke her and she looked at him with a soft loving look that she had often given to Bran but never to him before. He felt that something had occurred that day that had never happened before in his life.

Tomorrow he would start training her as Bran had trained her. He would learn how to handle her, and teach her to jump. Maybe he could do the display that Bran used to do at the local show. That had always been popular. Troy jumped over hurdles, went through a tunnel, found hidden purses and wallets, fetched things that people threw for her, sometimes over the hurdle, sometimes on the flat.

She would bring Bran his handkerchief, choosing it from a number of other hankies that lay on the ground. He lined up a number of children, clenched fists held out in front of them, and hid a biscuit in one child's hand, and Troy hunted along the line until she found it.

She would lie quite still while children ran round her, and Bran threw balls past her, never moving.

If only he could do something that Bran had

never done with her, he'd feel really grown-up instead of feeling like the baby of the family, who was never as clever as the others. Today had given him a glimpse into being himself, not trying to be like his brother.

It was a good feeling.

"How's the project going?" Grandma asked when he went down for cocoa and a biscuit just before bed. He let Troy out into the garden and waited for her before answering.

"I've been thinking about the way people used to live. The part their animals played in their lives. Backyard pigs in the last century. Wild pigs for the Normans. A time when nobody dreamed that men would walk on the moon or go into space or fly in aeroplanes."

"Those were impossible dreams, stories in books, when I was a child," Grandma said. "At least, going to the moon was. Aeroplanes were very different then. People didn't fly in them to go away on holidays. I remember seeing an airship when I was a little girl. It flew past my bedroom window, lit up all along its hull, if that's what they called it. And I heard music coming from it."

"Grandma Elizabeth told me a story about her grandmother," his mother said, coming into the room as Grandma Bridie was talking. "Her grandmother was born on a farm in Sussex. They smuggled brandy across from France. The Preventive Men came to inspect the farm, sure that they had hidden kegs there."

Troy walked across the room to lay her head in Sally Murray's lap, her eyes forlorn. Her ear hurt, and the stitches pulled. Sally stroked her as she spoke.

"Grandma Elizabeth's gran was three years old. She was wearing a long dress. They sat her on her potty on top of the cellar trapdoor. Nobody moved the little girl. The men didn't find the cellar entrance and went away."

Liam suddenly remembered a Kipling poem about smugglers.

"If your mother mends a coat that's cut about and tore, If the lining's wet and warm, don't you ask no more . . ." He said it aloud. Grandma smiled.

"I learned that at school, and said it for a verse-speaking competition. I've forgotten most of it. It was about the Gentlemen, as they called the smugglers. 'If you see a stable door, setting open wide, If you see a tired horse lying down inside . . .'"

"Down inside, down inside, down inside," Jed said rapidly. He had been listening intently, eating a piece of apple and now felt it time they noticed him. Everyone laughed and he joined in, his cackle continuing long beyond the others.

"Four and twenty ponies trotting through the dark," his father said from the doorway. "What brought this on?"

"Liam's project on the history of pigs," Grandma said, pouring cocoa from the pan into a mug. His father looked surprised as the poem didn't seem to have anything to do with pigs.

"I won't ask how," he said. "I've a feeling it would take too long telling. The only other bit I remember is 'a present from the Gentlemen along of being good'."

"'Brandy for the parson, baccy for the clerk, laces for a lady, letters for a spy'," Sally Murray said, her voice dreamy as if she were remembering a long ago past of her own when the poem had been familiar.

"Spy, spy, lady, lace," shouted Jed.

The room was warm, and Liam was sleepy. School tomorrow. He surprised himself by looking forward to giving in his project. He had taken immense care to write neatly and illustrated it with tiny sketches, with postcards and pictures of Roy's pigs. He had never done anything so well, or worked so hard. He had never felt so satisfied, and finding Tanya so that she was safe was an added bonus.

It had been a wonderful day, in spite of Troy's torn ear. His father said it would heal without a scar.

He realised, as he drifted towards sleep, Troy lying on his bedside rug, that it was the first time he hadn't missed the others. The family seemed to have closed up to be a unit again. When Jenna and the twins came home, they would almost be visitors, starting out in the world, taking off on their own unimaginable affairs after a few days or perhaps a week or so.

He had a long way to go, to prepare for that. His life had suddenly become intensely interesting. He would find out how to train Troy. He would put on the display with her this year at the Show. By the time he was Bran's age he would have money tucked away to start his own pig farm. He'd go to agricultural college first.

He would get a job as pig-farm manager, and learn from that, and then they would all see what he could do with his life. He had day-dreamed before. Now he would work to make those dreams reality.

His dreams that night were of Porgy jumping over hurdles, while Bess squealed in temper because she couldn't follow him. Troy suddenly flew in and attacked the little pig, and he couldn't drag her off. He was relieved to wake and find he had only been dreaming.

Oddly, the dream gave him a whale of an idea.

CHAPTER 10

Liam was not looking forward to school. Most of the lessons bored him, as he could see little point in them. If arithmetic had consisted of working out the cost of keeping pigs, of building sties, of the average vet bills during a pig's life, he might have seen some sense to it.

As it was, it never occurred to him to substitute the things he wanted to know for the figures in the obscure calculations he had to work out. The numbers produced both a headache and a mental block, and he battled with them daily.

"We've a new woodwork master," one of the boys in his class said. Woodwork was also boring and Liam took little notice until the first lesson began. Mr Dart was young with a ready grin.

"Boring old woodwork," he said, when the class was sitting waiting for him to begin. Everyone stared at him. "Making things very badly that nobody wants, yes?"

"Yes," they said, in chorus.

"So we'll make things people will want. Who's got small sisters?"

Several hands went up.

"So suppose you six make doll's houses for them for Christmas. As simple or as elaborate as you like. And maybe some of the others would like to make the furniture? We can wallpaper the inside, and paint the outside."

Within minutes everyone had something they wanted to make except Liam. He certainly didn't want to make doll's house furniture. He could hardly build a pigsty in the classroom. He sat silent, and the master suddenly realised he had one member of the group who seemed not to be taking part.

Tony Dart glanced at the diagrams as he passed each child. "Not too many tables. Let's be ambitious," he said. "I'll show you how to do the tricky bits.

"You are . . .?" he asked, walking over to

Liam. The rest were busy making plans, drawing up designs of what they wanted to do. Liam just sat. He wanted to make something for Porgy and Bess, but couldn't think of anything small that would be useful for a pig.

"I'm Liam Murray," Liam said, feeling he had no place anywhere in the class.

"What do you like doing?" The boy behind him sniggered. "All he ever thinks about is pigs. He even did his holiday project on pigs."

"That's interesting." Tony Dart sounded as if he really were interested. "I'd like to see it when you get it back. I can't offhand think of anything you could build in the classroom for pigs. Do you know any?"

"Lots. I go to the pig farm nearly every day." He wasn't going to say that he owned two pigs. That would mean more teasing.

"What else do you do?"

"I've got my brother's dog. She jumps hurdles."

"So what about making some of those? We can make her an agility course if you work hard enough and do it well enough. Hurdles and a catwalk and maybe you can find something to make a tunnel."

Some of the other children were listening.

"Anyone want to help make hurdles instead of doll's house furniture? And maybe when they're made, Liam will bring his dog and show us what she can do."

Five hands shot up.

"We've all got dogs, sir. Perhaps we can teach them to jump."

Hurdles were simple to make. There was a sudden new enthusiasm, with everyone eager for the woodwork afternoons. The local show was in mid-October, at half-term. Bran had always done a display with Troy then, but he had borrowed the equipment. He had asked Liam to do the display this year, as he didn't want to disappoint people.

The promise had worried Liam who was sure that he could never work Troy as his brother did.

Noah, when he heard about the plan, was enthusiastic, and he too made a few hurdles out of the wood lying in the barn. Painted red and white, they looked remarkably good. He put them on Roy's lawn at the front of the house. They had no time for flowers or vegetables, but the large patch of grass could be easily mown, and Roy wanted to present a tidy face to the world.

Once he had his museum and his farm trail planned, he would buy large tubs of flowers to put around the front door and along the edge of the path. Meanwhile Liam was welcome to train Troy there, provided he tidied the hurdles away when he had finished.

Troy loved jumping. Porgy, rather surprisingly, adored the big German Shepherd and followed her everywhere.

"He thinks he's a dog," Noah said, watching the two of them. They played together in the paddock and Porgy rarely let Troy out of his sight. Bess was less playful and preferred to hunt for tasty things to eat.

Porgy watched with fascination when he first saw Troy leap over the line of little jumps, which Noah had built so that they were no more than about twenty centimetres off the ground. The dog flew over them, one after another, her eyes alight with excitement.

Porgy walked over and sniffed the first, and then, to Noah's amazement and Liam's delight, he trotted over them too, his bright eyes shining with glee. Porgy loved people noticing him, and often played up, just to make everyone laugh.

"I could do a display with both of them in

October," Liam said eagerly. "We only have to have the right-sized hurdles. He can't jump as high as Troy."

At his next lesson, he stayed late and told his woodwork master about the pig.

"I'd like to see that," Tony Dart said. "Then we can design a course for Porgy too. What about a tunnel? If we have a number of hoops and some sailcloth I think we could construct a good one, big enough for the pig to go through, if you can teach him."

"He follows Troy everywhere." Liam was more excited than he could remember ever being before. Bess had no desire to jump, but amazingly she was learning to lie down and keep still in a stay position when he taught Troy and Porgy.

The local show was important to everyone. Once there had been a carnival, with flower floats, but that had been in August when there were so many other shows. They changed the date to October and had to change the style as there were not enough garden flowers to make the floats, and shop flowers were much too expensive.

There was country dancing, with the infant school and the senior citizens putting on their own displays. There was a harvest service and the vegetables and fruit that were brought went to the old people's home. There were classes for flower arranging and pottery and home-made toys, for jams and cakes and knitted goods, as well as displays of farm machinery and prize animals.

The Scouts and Guides and Cubs and Brownies from villages in the district all took part, sometimes singing, sometimes marching with a band. The local schools sent their choirs, and there were singing and music competitions as well.

Over the years the show had grown as people had more ideas, and enthusiasm built. The money collected from all the entries and the visitors went in prizes, with a great deal left over for various local charities.

Tony Dart determined they would have the best agility course for the dogs that anyone had ever seen. None of the boys knew about the pigs. Tony promised to keep that secret.

Liam began to enjoy school. His pig project was the best of them all and won a book token, which he spent on a book on animal feeding. It was called *The Nutrition of Farm Animals*. It was surprisingly difficult to understand. They needed minerals and vitamins, and special quantities of food according to what they were intended for.

There were maintenance diets and diets for breeding animals. There were invalid diets and diets for animals which had various deficiencies. There were obscure calculations on body weights. Maybe if people worked out how much food they needed according to how much they ought to weigh, they wouldn't get fat.

He was reading it in the kitchen one evening.

"It's an idea," Grandma said, baking mountains of cakes and biscuits which were to be sold on the day of the show. They went into the deep freeze into bags marked "Not for the family".

"Food, food, food, fat, fat fat," said Jed and pranced on his roost and shook his wings.

"Put his cover on, for goodness' sake," said Grandma. "I can't have feathers in the biscuits." Jed squawked with indignation as he was hidden in the dark. Liam went back to his book.

A working dog, like a sheepdog on the hills or a police dog patrolling, needed three times as much food as a pet dog. Gundogs had more food when working than they did in the winter when they were resting.

"You can give a horse too much oats and he goes quite crazy," his father said, when Liam commented that he'd never realised that animals needed less food when not being used for their work.

"Why?"

"Food makes energy and he isn't using his energy. So he'll be very awkward to handle. Ask Roy about his shire horses. They'll be rationed."

"Pigs aren't very active."

"Roy's foraging pigs are. They're using up a lot of energy hunting for their food. That keeps them much happier. Lying around in a sty all day doing nothing isn't good for them."

Woodwork classes buzzed with enthusiasm and excitement. The doll's houses began to look wonderful, with tiny furniture inside. One boy, who loved painting, made miniature pictures to hang on the walls.

There were a number of hurdles, the supports painted red, the slats for jumping painted white. Tony made several fancy ones, based on show-jumping fences.

One had a huge wooden "bone" to jump over.

The tunnel was tiresome to make, the sail-cloth heavy and awkward, the needles hard to use. But at last it was finished, with eight hoops to hold it up, and about a metre of cloth between each. It folded down into a fairly compact bundle.

Joe Sharp, whose father owned a small haulage business, promised transport to the field. Noah and Roy were bringing Porgy and Bess in the farm trailer.

The days sped by. Liam couldn't wait for his woodwork lessons. He was also making hurdles at home and Tony was helping him with a catwalk, consisting of planks that sloped up at either end, and it was joined by another wide enough for Porgy to walk along.

The children who didn't want to help with the doll's houses were busy with hurdles and weaving poles, and a frame for a tyre through which Troy could jump.

Liam was up early, setting hurdles on the lawn, teaching Troy to jump them when he told her and not when she chose, to lie down when he told her, to leap on to a little table, purposely built low so that Porgy could jump on to it too, though no one knew that.

He spent every weekend and two hours after school each day at Roy's farm, again with Troy and also with Porgy, while Bess happily lay still and watched, her bright eyes amused, as if she thoroughly enjoyed the show.

Liam's school provided the posters. One of the posters had a picture of Troy, copied from a photograph.

Porgy didn't like the tunnel, even when Troy went through first but he would follow her everywhere else, hurdling the little jumps neatly, an exuberant air about him that was almost a swagger as if he realised he was doing something unusual and very special.

Noah was teaching Liam how to handle his dog. He had once worked at a stables where the young horses were taught how to jump. He had many useful suggestions.

"Had an idea," Noah said the week before the show. He had a handful of pig pellets, and threw them into the tunnel, making sure that they fell at intervals. "Porgy hasn't been fed today. He's hungry." He put a bowl of pellets at one end.

"See if he'll go through now," Noah said.

Porgy had been watching from the edge of the lawn. He came, as Troy did, to a whistle, which Roy and Noah found extremely funny. Troy, lying still, as she had been told, watched as the pig went towards the tunnel. He stopped and looked at it. It was dark and for all he knew something nasty might be inside. Noah threw a few pellets in front of him, enticing him towards the entrance.

Hunger conquered fear. Porgy was very hungry indeed. He started to walk through the tunnel, eating as he went. He discovered, to his amazement, that nothing awful happened and at the other end was a big bowl of dinner.

"He can go through every day for his dinner," Noah said, satisfied that his scheme had worked. "He ought to be used to it by Saturday."

Saturday. The first thing Liam did when he woke was to draw the curtains and look out at the sky. Tuesday had been wet. Wednesday had been dull and cold. Thursday had been foggy. Friday blew a gale. The weather seemed determined to put on its worst face, but at least the wind dried the show field.

Everyone in the family was taking part. Lois

was judging to find the rabbit with the twitchiest nose. Romana was looking for the best-dressed teddy bear. She herself had entered the embroidery class with a christening robe of silk and lace covered in tiny white flowers, which would then be auctioned.

Grandma Bridie was helping in the tea tent. His mother had agreed to pick out the prettiest baby and wished she hadn't as it would probably cause a war among her young mothers. Maybe doctors shouldn't judge their patients, Grandma said, but it was too late to back out. Somebody had to win, but an awful lot had to lose.

Josh Murray was judging the most unusual pet. One of the boys had a young python, and as it was the only one, he was certain he would win.

Liam and Noah and Roy and Tony Dart were busy putting up the agility apparatus. The local nursery was lending them tubs of plants to decorate the show field. Liam hoped the pigs wouldn't eat them. Suppose Porgy refused to go through the tunnel, or rushed off to lie beside Bess, or wouldn't jump? Suppose Troy was distracted by other dogs and went to play?

It was a bright day, with a small wind that

156

troubled the grass, but did not cause problems. It was too good to be true.

Liam was at the show field by eight o'clock, helping Tony Dart put a ring up and set out the apparatus. Noah and Roy arrived soon after, with Porgy and Bess comfortably settled on straw in the trailer.

Troy lay at the side of the ring, watching, aware that she was going to perform. She adored jumping, even more than tracking. Liam had new jeans and a sweatshirt on which Romana had embroidered a German Shepherd's head. He wondered if Bran had felt as nervous. They had to wait several hours before their turn came.

There were small clouds in the sky. If only they didn't build into rain.

"Biggest show we've ever had," Roy said, looking at the marquees and the tables and benches. The field was immense, as it had several football pitches on it. The goal posts looked out of place, with cars parked at the edge of the field, and tables beneath them, covered in goods for sale.

Liam went from one table to another, Troy on her lead. Books. Children's gloves and socks. Leads and collars for dogs. He looked at them, but none of them were strong enough for his dog.

"There's a very unusual display this morning," Tony Dart said. "Just before yours. The Head has a friend with a trained hawk. He's going to fly it. A peregrine falcon."

Liam had just bought a hot dog and felt his appetite drain away. It would take away any interest anyone had in his display. A hawk was much more unusual. He wished he'd never said he'd do it.

He watched the bird fly high, soaring into the sun. The falconer swung a lure, made of rook's feathers fastened to a string. The bird plunged, diving through the air, to take hold and grip, and be rewarded with a slice of raw meat.

It was a beautiful bird, but Liam did not dare go near in case Troy upset it. It might not like dogs and he was not sure what she would make of the falcon.

Waiting was horrible.

The minutes crawled by. They were due on at two, immediately after lunch. Would anyone stay? Would anyone watch? The children in his class would, as they felt involved, having made so many of the hurdles and also the red and

158

white weaving poles. Those had to be set wide apart, or Porgy couldn't manage them as his body wouldn't bend like Troy's.

By lunchtime there were clouds across the sun. If only it didn't rain. Jumping on wet ground was risky and he couldn't very well cancel the display. The show field was packed. Everyone in the village had come and brought their relatives, and there were people from the nearby town.

He went into the refreshment tent. Grandma handed him a ham sandwich and a plastic beaker of tea, but he found it hard to swallow. Half-past one. Only half an hour to wait. He knew he was going to make a fool of himself. Lois's husband was taking photographs, and positioned himself near the ring.

Tony Dart was already beside the microphone as he was going to do the commentary. He grinned at Liam.

"Got butterflies?"

"Tropical ones, the size of that falcon," Liam said. Noah had manoeuvred the trailer into position.

Tony began to speak, his voice echoing over the show field.

"Ladies and gentlemen, boys and girls, may

I have your attention please. You are about to see something unique in the history of this show. Liam Murray has not only trained his German Shepherd dog to jump, but he has another animal athlete for you. A very surprising and unusual one. If you want to see the show of a lifetime, walk up. Walk up. Walk up."

Liam went into the ring, Troy beside him. His father stood behind Tony, and beside him was the mayor, wearing his chain of office. The mayor was one of his father's clients. He had an Irish Wolfhound named Shannon.

Liam had to concentrate. Why on earth had he been such an idiot as to imagine he could do this? Not even his parents knew about the pigs.

His pocket was full of pig pellets and Porgy was to go through the tunnel first. It was carefully laid with a trail of food for him. Troy would follow happily. She didn't need any encouragement. He might have to discourage her from turning round and going back again.

The band struck up with a merry little tune so that soon everyone was humming. There was a roll of drums.

"Ladies and gentlemen, I present to you

Liam Murray and Troy and Porgy and Bess, his performing pigs."

There was a low murmur of laughter. Liam saw his father's eyebrows disappear almost into his hair and a very odd expression on the mayor's face. Noah opened the trailer.

Liam forgot everything around him. Time to act. He did not notice Tony's commentary. He whistled and the pigs trotted towards him. Bess lay down as soon as she was told, at the corner of the ring.

"Please make sure all dogs are on the lead," said Tony. "We don't want the display interrupted. The pigs might not like strange dogs around them."

A buzz went round the show field – "There are performing pigs," – and more and more people flocked to see.

"Now," said Liam, and off Troy went, over four hurdles, and on to the table, then on to the ground and lay down as Porgy followed her, his neat little trotters clearing the jumps with inches to spare. He jumped on to the table and waited for Troy to clear the little water jump, go through two tyres and then the weaving poles. Porgy waited until Liam had sent Troy right across the ring to lie down beside Bess, and then he started off. The tyre was difficult and not a jump he liked, but Liam was ready at the other side, a pig pellet hidden in his hand. Porgy shot through the tyre, took the pellet and weaved through the poles.

The planks on the catwalk had little ridges on them to prevent the animals slipping. There was a gasp as Porgy trotted up the plank and stood quite still on the top of the walk, looking around him.

Liam thought, for one horrible moment, that he didn't intend to come down, but, with a sudden air of decision, he trotted on, and down the other side, while Troy ran over.

Porgy lay beside Bess while Troy fetched a toy rabbit that Romana had made for her, carried it down the field and presented it to Liam.

"Bring out your handkerchiefs, if you use them," Tony said. Roy took hankies from the people who offered them and Liam put his down among twenty others. Noah held Troy so that she couldn't see where the handkerchief was placed.

Troy trotted over, smelled each one, picked Liam's up, and brought it back to him. She put her head on one side when people clapped.

Liam was glad that Noah had insisted they did clap the animals when practising, in case the sound upset them. Though the three of them had never made as much noise as this.

At the far side of the ring there were twenty little pyramids made of plastic, with open ends inside which things could be hidden.

Roy put a cooked sausage under one of the pyramids and Liam sent Troy to find it.

"She might eat it," Tony said to the crowd. "We hope she won't."

That had been one of Bran's tricks. Troy knew it well, and she brought the sausage back to Liam who broke it in two and gave it to her to eat.

Now it was Porgy's turn.

"Porgy loves chocolate," Tony said. "We can't expect him to carry it back to us, but he'll tell Liam where it's hidden, three times. He's never wrong. He can't see the chocolate. He's going to find it by smell."

Tony called a small girl from the audience and gave her a chocolate to hide.

"It's under number seventeen," Tony said. Each pyramid had a number on it.

Porgy trotted along the line, sniffing intently. When he reached number seventeen he pushed at it and turned to look at Liam, who gave the pig his reward. Porgy found the chocolates hidden under number six and number thirteen with equal ease.

Now for the tunnel. Porgy had been watching it with interest, knowing what lay inside. Liam whistled to him and he trotted towards it, but his eye was distracted. A child at the edge of the ring was eating a big red apple. Porgy loved apples.

Before Liam could stop him he ran across the ring, snatched the apple and stood munching it. The child cried out in dismay, then laughed, and Liam whistled.

"Tunnel," he said, and led Porgy forward, the little pig happily following him, scenting the pellets hidden in Liam's hand. Porgy caught the scent of pig food and was at once inside, munching as he went. At the end he came out and trotted over to the table and jumped on to it again.

Troy ran towards the tunnel and then had a thought of her own. Instead of going into it she jumped over it. Everyone laughed. Liam thought quickly and sent her over and back, over and back, all the way along it and then through from the other end.

He drew a deep breath. No one realised she had done wrong and Tony lifted up his thumb in triumph.

Liam put Troy on the lead and began to heel her in a pattern. Forward, right, left, circle. Beside him, as close as he could get to the big dog, trotted Porgy, also doing heel-work. The roars of laughter and clapping followed them as they walked.

In the centre of the ring was a cloth covering a large board, which they used as the centre-piece of their work.

Slowly, walking as if they were at a funeral. Fast, racing as if they had a train to catch. Without any commands at all, both dog and pig followed Liam's movements and ended lying down beside him.

Liam whistled to Bess, who now came into the act.

This was her big moment. She was still a small pig, much smaller than Porgy and every-one loved her. She picked up the rope that lay on the ground, settling it firmly in her mouth, and walked away with it. The cloth fell off, revealing a painted message that read,

THE END. WE HOPE YOU HAVE ENJOYED US.

Liam thought the applause would never stop. He was aware of cameras flashing, and that someone had a video recorder.

Noah enticed the pigs into the trailer, using their dinner as their reward, and drove them across to a quiet part of the field, where he parked again.

"I'm speechless," his father said. "Whatever made you think of that?"

"Porgy and Bess are mine. Roy gave me Bess and I bought Porgy with some of my birthday money. When I started training Troy at the farm, Porgy began to follow her. He loves jumping."

"What are you going to do with them?"

"Breed from both of them. Bess will make a good brood sow, Noah says, and Porgy is the only boar at stud that might have progeny that can be sold for jumping."

Liam was surrounded by boys and girls from his school, all wanting to stroke Troy, and to ask about the pigs. Liam had an idea he wanted to discuss with Tony Dart. He put Troy in his father's Land Rover to rest and went into the tea tent.

"Well done," Tony said, putting in front of him a plate of ham salad. "You've earned that. That was a splendid bit of quick thinking when Troy went over the tunnel instead of through."

Liam had been thinking for days. He wanted to thank Roy for all the trouble he had gone to for them, and also for giving him Bess and keeping his pigs on the farm. He had an idea, but it would need a lot of planning and he wasn't even sure that it was a good idea. Maybe Tony Dart could help him work it out and tell him if he thought it wrong. Tony was only Tony when they met outside school. In class he was always Mr Dart. Sometimes it was hard to remember. "Listen," Liam said and then thought again. Maybe it was daft.

"Can't listen if you don't talk," Tony said.

"Roy has problems on the farm. With people who leave gates open. With people who dump litter. With children that come to the yard at times and tease the animals. Suppose the school adopted the farm? Made it our school farm? We could have groups go round on Roy's farm trail and get everyone involved in making it a success. A school farm to teach everyone what farming is about. Maybe they'd be interested, now they've seen the pigs. Do you think the Head would agree?"

Tony was looking over Liam's shoulder, his eyes amused. Liam looked round and blushed a fiery red and swallowed. He hadn't seen his headmaster, who had come to congratulate him. The Head could be terrifying and Liam was very much in awe of him.

"I should think the Head might agree," he said, smiling. "It sounds to me like one of the best ideas I've ever heard. It might not have worked even yesterday, but everyone is fascinated by your pigs and wants to know how they've been trained. What about Mr Marsh? Would he agree?"

"I'm sure he would," Liam said. "He's always saying people ought to know more about farming and need to be taught about the countryside. That's the whole point of his farm trail. It isn't ready yet but suppose Mr Dart took his woodwork classes up there and they worked on it, like a project? It would be the most practical project anyone has ever done. They could repair sties and maybe even build new ones, make arks for the outdoor pigs, and there are always fences to mend."

Liam was overcome with enthusiasm, and forgot his shyness.

"The art classes could do the notices. The woodwork class can make little boards that the art people can paint, with the animals' names on them and what breeds they are."

"We could help with the museum and maybe the school could run a farm shop," Tony Dart said. "Stock it and take it in turns to look after it. Maybe some of the parents would be interested and come and do teas."

"Where's this wonderful farm?" Roy asked, amusement in his voice. Liam hadn't seen him come in.

"Your farm," Liam said. "It would work, wouldn't it?"

"It's something I've had in mind but not known quite how to get off the ground, or which school to ask to help me," Roy said. "We could have other schools come on coach trips."

"I have a desk-top publishing unit at home," Tony Dart said. "I can bring it into school and we can set up our own print shop. Do headed notepaper and the art classes can design letter-heads. We can run off a whole lot of leaflets about Roy's farm and mail them to other

schools and put them in libraries and hotels."
They were all talking at once, ideas spilling
over. Liam felt as if he would never stop
grinning. Life was suddenly more exciting than
he had ever known. He could see the future
spreading out before him, with ideas of all
kinds coming to fruition. His head was brim-
ming over with plans. He was growing up and
being thirteen was different after all. He'd
never had these sorts of ideas when he was only
twelve.

He couldn't wait to get home and write his
ideas down before they vanished from his head.
He felt nine miles high, and even higher that
night when he discovered that the man with
the camcorder had sent the video to the tele-
vision studio. There, for all the nation to see,
was Liam with Porgy and Troy, and Bess lying
quietly in the corner.

The best part of the day was still to come.

Bran rang at ten o'clock.

"Well done, little brother," he said. "I saw
the news. You're growing up fast. I'd never
have thought of that in a million years. I'm
giving you Troy, as I won't be able to have her
as mine again."

It was the best present he had ever had,

better even than the pigs, as he and Troy were now partners, working together. They belonged.

He sat in the kitchen making notes until his father sent him off to bed.

Jed had been quiet all evening, but as Liam went upstairs the bird shouted after him.

"Night night, Liam. Sleep tight, Liam. Life's what you make it if it doesn't make you."

Liam chuckled. He knew that night when he was in bed that he would never have another day to treasure like this. He felt that he had come a very long way in the last few weeks and maybe that was what being thirteen was really about. It was the start of his future. It had set a pattern for the rest of his life. Jed had been trying to repeat Noah's maxim.

"Life's what you make it. Nobody owes you a living, young Liam, so get out and look about you and see what there is to do and do it."

He was almost asleep when his father put his head round the door.

"I've been worried about you, but not any more. I think, of the four, you might go the furthest. I was talking to Roy at the show and he reckons by the time you're twenty-one you'll have made enough money from breeding pigs to buy yourself a partnership with him. He has no heirs, so the farm might one day be yours. Think about it, son."

The House of Secrets, with secrets hidden for the future, still coming to light. Jed confusedly called it the House of Dreams. Perhaps it was that too.

Liam wished that Bran was there so that he could tell his brother how wonderful his find had been. Had Bran not seen it that long-ago day, they might never have come to their new home. He no longer wished that he were as old as the rest of the family. He needed time, to grow, to learn, to build for his own future.

The future that was there, to grasp.

Troy nosed him and curled up beside his bed, and he listened to her quiet breathing. Then he too fell asleep and dreamed of Romana promising them all three wishes that would come true.

"I don't need them," he said in his dream. "Mine are already coming true."

Homecoming by Cynthia Voigt
£3.50

Dicey made her announcement to James, Sammy and Maybeth: "We're going to have to walk all the way to Bridgeport." But they had no money and the whole world was arranged for people who had money – or rather, for adults who had money. The world was arranged against kids. Well, she could handle it. She'd have to. Somehow.

Dicey's Song by Cynthia Voigt
£3.50

Still troubled about her mother, and anxious about the three younger children, Dicey seems to have no time for growing up – until an incident at school shows her what to do.

A Solitary Blue by Cynthia Voigt
£3.50

Jeff has always been a loner, ever since his mother walked out, leaving him with his taciturn and distant father. Then his mother invites him to Charleston. For one glorious summer, Jeff is happy, before his dreams are shattered.

The Runner by Cynthia Voigt
£3.50

Bullet Tillerman has little interest in anyone or anything except running. But this is the 1960s, and with racial war at home and the Vietnam War abroad, Bullet's beliefs have to change, particularly when he's asked to coach a new black runner at the school.

Some Other War
Linda Newbery

Seventeen-year-old twins Jack and Alice have their lives mapped out. Jack is a stable lad at the Morlands' country house, and Alice is chambermaid to Madeleine Morland. Had it not been for the First World War, they might have stayed there all their lives. But the war changed many things, and brought Jack and Alice independence from the rigid social structure of the times.

Jack joins up with the first flush of enthusiasm, and is sent to the trenches. Alice continues at the Morlands', but as the casualties mount up and it becomes obvious the war will not be over by Christmas, she feels she must do something to help and begins working as a nurse.

Linda Newbery's novel accurately and sympathetically portrays life at the time of the Great War through the eyes of young people.

£3.99

The Indian in the Cupboard
by Lynne Reid Banks

When Omri is given a toy Indian and a small cupboard for his birthday, it seems natural to keep the Indian safely in the cupboard. And when, amazingly, the little man comes to life, Omri is thrilled at the thought of all the wonderful games they can play. It isn't long, though, before he realises that being responsible for another human being, no matter how small, is no laughing matter...

Return of the Indian by Lynne Reid Banks

Just over a year after Omri and his best friend, Patrick, have renounced the alarming power of bringing their model people to life, the boys find the temptation quite irresistible. But this time, the boys discover the added excitement of transporting themselves to a different place and time, with dangerous results.

The Secret of the Indian
by Lynne Reid Banks

After a terrible battle, many of Little Bull's warriors are wounded. Omri must get them medical help, but he must also protect the secret of the Indian. When Patrick goes back in time to the Wild West and falls into terrible danger, keeping the secret safe becomes even more difficult for Omri.

All at £3.99

Order Form

To order direct from the publishers, just make a list of the titles you want and fill in the form below:

Name ....

Address ....

....

....

Send to: Dept 6, HarperCollins Publishers Ltd, Westerhill Road, Bishopbriggs, Glasgow G64 2QT.

Please enclose a cheque or postal order to the value of the cover price, plus:

UK & BFPO: Add £1.00 for the first book, and 25p per copy for each addition book ordered.

Overseas and Eire: Add £2.95 service charge. Books will be sent by surface mail but quotes for airmail despatch will be given on request.

A 24-hour telephone ordering service is avail-able to Visa and Access card holders: 041-772 2281